SEA CHASE

The Adventures of Young John Quincy Adams
Book 1

by

John Braddock

CONTENTS

Though based on a true story and real characters, this is a work of fiction and of the author's imagination.

Prologue
June 1775

When the sun was past its height, Johnny Adams scrambled up a hill south of Boston. Reaching the top, he shielded his gray eyes and looked north. The morning mist had burned off. There was no breeze from the sea. The air was hot and clear.

On the hill beyond Boston, there was a flicker of fire. A dark cloud of smoke hung above it, like it was waiting for something.

"What's the smoke from?" asked Joey Warren as he crested the hill.

"Red Coats," said Johnny as he watched what looked like discolored rocks on the far beach. The rocks were moving. "They're burning Charlestown."

"Now they burn Charlestown?" exclaimed Johnny's mother, arriving with her skirt in her hands. Johnny looked like his mother, people said. He had a nose straight and pointed and tall cheeks that rounded to a neat chin. "Must the Red Coats destroy everything?"

"Why Charlestown, Mamma?" asked Johnny's older sister Nabby, long braids bouncing. "Why would the British burn it?"

"Because our men stand above it on Bunker Hill.

See there? Below Bunker Hill is Charlestown. And below Charlestown are the Red Coats. On the beach just under the smoke. They're getting ready to attack."

Joey said quietly, "My father is there."

"Your father is not there, Joey," said Johnny's mother quickly. "He went to organize the militia elsewhere."

While Dr. Joseph Warren led the militia, Joey Warren was staying on the Adams farm in Braintree. With the Adams' father also away at the Continental Congress, Joey was a welcome help with the work on the farm.

"Begging your pardon, Mrs. Adams," said Joey firmly. "He is there. If there's to be a fight, he'll be there. He wouldn't miss a fight against the Red Coats."

Johnny's mother slipped an arm around Joey's shoulders. "If you're right, pray for his safety."

"He said not to," said Joey matter-of-factly. "He said to pray he does the right thing, regardless of safety."

Johnny rubbed the scars on his finger. They were scars that Joey's father had made when it could have been worse.

It began with a rabbit startling the plow mule. The mule bolted with Johnny's hand in the leather and dragged Johnny to the end of the pasture. When Johnny pulled his finger free from the straps, it was bloody and twisted.

The village doctor shook his head at the sight. "It

must be amputated," he said.

"No! Please don't! Please!" pleaded Johnny.

But the doctor only sharpened his knives.

"Mamma, please!" Johnny had cried. "Please don't let him!"

The doctor's blade was nearly to Johnny's finger when his mother said, "Stop! Dr. Warren will see it before Johnny goes through life with nine fingers."

The village doctor huffed. "Dr. Warren? My expertise and knowledge of medical –"

"We thank you and will pay for your time, doctor," interrupted Johnny's mother. "But we will wait for Dr. Warren."

When Dr. Warren saw Johnny's finger, he shook his head like the village doctor had done. But he had a different answer. "I can fix it, Johnny, but it will be a painful thing. The stitches must be tight. The pain would be less if I cut it off."

"You – you can save it?" Johnny stuttered through white lips.

"If you can stand the pain," answered Dr. Warren.

Johnny stretched out his mangled finger. "Please – please do it."

Johnny screamed when Dr. Warren's metal pincers pulled the first piece of skin from the muscle. Then the needle went deep. The whole world felt on fire.

Johnny tried to separate himself from his finger, to imagine it was someone else's. But each pull of the thread brought him back. When Dr. Warren finally stopped, Johnny was shaking.

Then Dr. Warren poured alcohol on the wound, and Johnny passed out.

When Dr. Warren came back to remove the last bandage, white scars were all over the puffy skin.

"You'll have those scars the rest of your life," said Dr. Warren with a pat on Johnny's shoulder. "But you should be proud. Count them as a reminder that you bore the pain, even as a boy. A thing few men will do."

Johnny held his scarred finger against the smoky sky over Bunker Hill. Was Dr. Warren really there? Was he commanding the cannons? Ordering the soldiers? Giving a speech?

Johnny's mother caught her breath. In the distance, the rocky mass of Red Coats swarmed up the hill. They climbed like a landslide going the wrong way. Some got ahead, then others passed them. The Red Coats moved faster and faster and disappeared into the smoke.

The world went quiet.

Johnny looked at his mother. "When will something happen?"

A thousand flashes erupted on the distant hill.

A boom rumbled like thunder.

Johnny's mother put a hand on Johnny's shoulder and squeezed.

"What's happening?" asked Johnny. "What do you see?" His mother ignored Johnny and stared at Bunker Hill.

Out of the smoke dropped Red Coats in twos and

threes. Then a dozen. Then hundreds. They rolled down to the beach.

"Huzzah, Huzzah!" shouted Joey, relief on his face. "We've beaten them back! Just like Lexington and Concord! The Red Coats can't beat us!"

Johnny's mother pointed to the bottom of the hill. "We haven't won yet, Joey. The Red Coats gather again."

Behind them a voice called out, "What news of the rebellion, Mrs. Adams?" A stallion deposited a short bald man with a stomach covered in brass buttons. His skinny legs hit the ground and bent like willow branches under his weight. Brushing off his coat, he said, "Well?"

"Mr. Hanford," said Johnny's mother. "You will be disappointed. Our patriots have beaten back the Red Coats."

"Mrs. Adams, you have me wrong," said Mr. Hanford, pulling an eyepiece from his saddlebag. "I want only peace. Your husband and the rebels in Philadelphia are starting a foolish war against King George. Men are meant to serve a king."

Johnny burst out angrily, "Men are meant to be free! We will be free!"

"Quiet, Johnny," said Johnny's mother quickly. "You must show respect for Mr. Hanford, no matter his opinions."

"But —" started Johnny.

"You see!" exclaimed Mr. Hanford. "The King's men attack!"

Thousands of Red Coats ran up the hill again, rifles glinting through the smoke.

Time slowed. Seconds ticked.

Johnny tried not to blink.

Suddenly, light filled the smoke. Another boom shook the air.

Down the hill dropped the Red Coats, fewer this time. An officer rode through them, his sword flashing in the air.

"Mr. Hanford," said Johnny's mother with an edge Johnny had never heard before. "The king is a tyrant. The peace you want is the peace of slaves who do not upset their master. We will not be slaves. Our rebels would rather die than live under the king's boot."

Mr. Hanford kept his gaze on the battle. "I meant no offense, Mrs. Adams. I mean only to say that King George, for good or bad, will win this war. It's best to be on the winning side. He has offered a pardon to all who lay down their arms."

"Not to all, Mr. Hanford," answered Johnny's mother. "He has sworn to arrest and execute my husband."

Mr. Hanford ignored her. "There go the Red Coats again!"

"You see, Mr. Hanford," said Johnny's mother. "King George cares nothing for life. He sends his Red Coats to die against our guns."

Johnny braced for another flash, for another boom to roll across the water.

But there was no flash. There was no boom.

Only lonely pinpricks of light. Like the last sparks of a dying fire. A weak clash sounded.

Beyond the smoke, dark-coated men ran backward, then more. They stopped and fired and sprinted away. A small group knotted together and held their ground, letting others escape.

"Your rebels are retreating! They have lost Bunker Hill!" said Mr. Hanford. "The king has more Red Coats than you have rebels. His soldiers will always overwhelm converted farmers, blacksmiths and merchants. If you want peace, you must bow to the king."

"We will not!" said Johnny's mother angrily. "King George can send a million Red Coats and thousands of ships and cannons. We will die rather than be slaves! We will be free!"

An old mare carried a young man down the dark road to Braintree. Each sway brought a fresh gasp of pain and blood from the wound on his neck. He saw a candle in the window at the Hanford house and kept going. He would get no help there.

A light flickered at the Adams farm. Robert urged the old mare toward it. He would get help from Mrs. Adams.

The young man's weak knock brought a suspicious, "Yes?"

He tried to answer but only a grunt came out.

The door opened.

"Robert, is that you?" asked Abigail Adams. "What happened? Where are you hurt? Nabby, Johnny, Joey, come quick!" Mrs. Adams gave instructions. "Johnny, Joey, put your arms under Robert's shoulders – that's right. Watch his neck. Nabby, fetch a towel and put the kettle on. Set him down on the table. Carefully!"

Robert sagged. Joey and Johnny caught him and lifted him to the table.

Nabby returned with a wet towel and dabbed at Robert's neck. Robert winced. He tightened his jaw and tried to look courageous.

"The wound's not deep," said Mrs. Adams, washing blood from her hands. "But you'll need some stitches to close it. Dr. Warren can sew it when he comes."

"Ma'am, Mrs. Adams," said Robert through his teeth. "If you don't mind, we'll need to call another doctor. Dr. Warren was killed."

"Killed?" said Johnny's mother, with a quick glance at Joey. "That's – that's impossible. He was away from Bunker Hill. Organizing the militia."

"He was there, Mrs. Adams, as much as I was. Next to me, in the thick of the fight."

Johnny, his mother and sister looked at Joey. "Oh, Joey," said Johnny's mother.

Joey pushed toward Robert, his eyes filling. "Please, what – what happened?"

"He died saving the rest of us – that's what happened," said Robert. "After the second volley, there was only enough powder for a few guns. We spread them along the line, hoping to frighten the Red Coats into running away. But they feared their officers' swords more than us. They rushed at us with knives.

"With the powder gone, we were no match. We had to retreat. But Dr. Warren wouldn't fall back. He stood his ground against the hundreds of British, using his pistols. He stopped the Red Coats, almost by himself, Mrs. Adams. He held them off, so we could escape. Then he fell."

Johnny's mother wrapped Joey in her arms. "Oh, Joey, I'm so sorry. Your father."

Robert craned his bleeding neck toward Joey. "Oh, I didn't know. Your father - if not for Dr. Warren – if not for him – none of us would have survived."

Joey's eyes glistened. "He did the right thing."

Johnny felt a dark, sickening blackness rise in his chest. It climbed to his throat and pushed into his head. It filled his skull. He saw flashes of light.

Johnny ran his thumb across his scarred finger.

Dr. Warren had stood. He had fought the British when everyone else was running. He had been courageous. He had saved hundreds of others.

Johnny wanted to do something.

Anything.

What could he do?

"I often regretted that I had brought my Son with me . . . Fully sensible of our Danger, he was constantly endeavouring to bear up under it with a manly courage."

The Autobiography of John Adams

Chapter One
February 1778

Johnny's stomach was rolling like the ship. Side to side. Up and down. Shuddering when it hit a wave.

His stomach wanted to be back on land. Somewhere stable. Somewhere still. Anywhere but on a ship.

The ship rose on a wave, and Johnny tipped out of the hammock. He landed next to his father's empty hammock. The floor shifted. Johnny lost his balance and nearly fell into the wall.

Johnny grabbed his father's desk. Steadying himself, he felt in the dark for the cabin wall and found the door. Hand on the handle, his stomach moved again. His dinner was coming up.

He took a deep breath and hurried into the hallway.

The companion hatch bounced above. The ladder

underneath was slick with sea spray. Johnny balanced himself and went up a step. Then another. He pushed the hatch open and his face met the wind.

Johnny filled his lungs with ocean air. His stomach stopped rolling. He sat on the top rung breathing with relief.

Around him was blackness. The lanterns had been darkened to hide from British ships.

But there were sounds. Seagulls screeched. Sails whipped in the wind. Timber creaked under their strain. Waves crashed against the hull. Sailors shouted to be heard.

A large wave hit the ship, and everything shuddered again. A warm sick feeling climbed in Johnny's throat.

Johnny staggered past a snickering sailor. He dodged three others pulling a rope. He went past two ropes hanging from a spar. Finally, he found the rail.

Beyond was the white-spotted ocean and fog above it.

A knot in his stomach loosened. Then it tightened again.

Everything came up. Everything his mother had given him the night before. Everything he had eaten and drank. Everything.

Everything flew into the sea.

His stomach convulsed again and again until nothing was left.

Exhausted, Johnny collapsed behind a barrel. He closed his eyes and pretended everything was still.

That everything was quiet. That everything was over. That he was back on the farm in Braintree.

A sailor's rough whisper sounded behind him. Johnny tried to ignore it. But the man spoke again. He said, "Have you found them?"

Found what? thought Johnny. What was he supposed to find? Johnny tried to sit up on his elbow.

But the man wasn't talking to him. "Not yet," answered a second voice. There was fear in it mixed with caution and worry.

A wave crashed again, drowning out the voices. When it was quiet, the first voice was saying, ". . . the strongbox?"

The second answered, "I haven't found the key."

"Did you see if the cabin boy has one?"

"If he has one, how will I get it? He stays close to the captain all of the time."

Johnny's stomach moved again. But there was nothing left to lose, so he stayed where he was.

"Find the key," said the first voice. "And when you've found the secret plans, don't steal them. Leave them be. Very important you leave them be. Understand?"

There was a quake in the second one's voice. "You'll vouch for me when they come?"

"Aye," said the first one. "And you'll be rewarded. I've got a letter from Lord North himself. They'll have no doubt."

Lord who? Lord South? Is that what the man said? No . . . Lord West? What were they talking about?

Plans? Who were these men?

Johnny got to his elbows. Pulled his feet under him. Braced himself. Stood up.

The two men were gone.

Or maybe they weren't. Maybe they were right in front of him. There were probably a hundred sailors on the deck, but Johnny couldn't see them. He could only hear them. He could hear them moving in the ropes. Shimmying up masts. Swinging like squirrels.

The two men had been talking about a strongbox. Secret plans. A reward for stealing them. And a Lord who would pay.

British spies.

What were the secret plans? His father's plans? His father was going to France to get help for the Revolution. But that wasn't a secret. Everyone knew it. And it wasn't the kind of plan that could be stolen.

What secret plans were they looking for?

"Johnny!" came a cheery voice. "That's a green face you've got. Let me get you back to your cabin."

"Mr. Griffin," said Johnny. "There's something – I – I just heard something. Sailors talking about a strongbox and a Lord and secret plans."

Mr. Griffin put an arm under Johnny. "Put your arm over my shoulder, Johnny. I'll help you to your cabin. Don't you worry. Sailors are always talking. And it's always foolishness."

"But–" started Johnny. "There was more to it. Stealing it. And a reward."

Mr. Griffin laughed a little too loudly. At Johnny's

look, he got quiet. "Could be that your stomach is messing with your head. Get yourself back to bed. We'll see how you feel in the morning."

Johnny staggered back to his swinging hammock. He climbed in and thought about what he heard.

A Lord. A strongbox. A key. Plans.

That's what he heard.

He knew what he heard.

They were spies.

British spies.

They had to be.

After General Washington's army retook Bunker Hill, the British had left Boston. But they hadn't left America. They moved their headquarters to the port at New York. From there, they set up blockades along the coast. They raided coastal towns. Their ships harassed every American ship that tried to sail.

American ships that broke the blockade were chased by British ships. Like rabbits escaping sprinting wolves. The British ships were faster with more guns and caught American ships every week.

Desperate for help, the Congress had turned to France. They had sent Ben Franklin to France to ask for help, but that was two years ago. No French ships had come. The French king must have told Ben Franklin no.

The British ships continued to raid and chase the American ships that sailed.

The Congress decided another man sent to France might convince the French king to send help:

Johnny's father. Together, John Adams and Ben Franklin would get French help, the Congress hoped. The French king would send ships and weapons. Maybe French soldiers, too.

That was why Johnny and his father were sailing to France.

But that was all they were doing, as far as Johnny knew.

Unless his father hadn't told him. Unless there was a secret plan for getting French help.

What could it be?

Johnny wanted to ask his father, but his father wasn't there.

It had been foggy and dark when they boarded the ship. The captain had given the order to lift anchor immediately. All sails had been raised. They had speeded past the shoals and tiny islands off the Massachusetts coast. They wanted to reach open ocean before the British ships saw them.

Johnny's stomach had revolted, and his father wasn't back from where he had gone. The captain's cabin?

The sounds of the ship quieted. Johnny decided to ask his father in the morning about the secret plans.

Johnny drifted off to sleep.

The morning's warm gray sun came through the porthole and landed on Johnny's face.

The warmth felt like a fly, and his hand tried to swat it away. Instead, he slapped his face and woke himself up. Blinking, Johnny lifted his head. It threw off his balance. His hammock turned sideways.

Below him, his father's hammock was still empty. Johnny swung back and forth until he could turn himself. Right side up again, Johnny stared at the ceiling.

He tried to remember what had been so important the night before. There had been something. Something important. But Mr. Griffin thought it wasn't. Or acted like he thought it wasn't. But it was important. Secret plans? A strongbox? A Lord? That was it!

Johnny swung his legs over and jumped softly to the floor. He stood for a moment to see what his empty stomach would do. It did nothing, so he put his clothes on. He wondered where his father was. He wanted to tell him what he heard. To ask about secret plans.

But first, he had to be sure. Johnny decided to retrace his steps. To find the barrel he had been behind. To find where the sailors he heard would have stood. Just to be sure.

Johnny poked his head into the sunlight on the quarterdeck and saw what had been covered by fog the night before.

A whirlwind of sailors.

Some were tall. Most were short. Many were furry as squirrels, with chins and forearms thick with hair.

All were strong and moving with speed.

Johnny tried to make sense of it. He tracked one sailor from deck to mast to rope. But he lost him as he went behind a sail. Johnny watched another climb to the forecastle, go up the foremast and tighten a rope.

Johnny rubbed his eyes and followed three more. They went from bow to stern. To the higher deck at the back of the boat. Where there was a man steering a wheel.

So much happening. So much work to push a ship through the sea.

But where was he last night? Where was the rail he went to? Where was the barrel he sat behind when he heard the voices?

Before he could find them, a voice said, "Are you Johnny Adams?"

Chapter Two

Three boys appeared.

The first was older than Johnny. He was in his late teens and tall. His long nose made it look like he was running even when he was standing still. Pale skin was tight over sharp cheeks. Dark hair was swept back and tied fashionably in a ponytail.

The second boy was shorter than the first boy but much larger. He had a round belly barely contained by a dirty coat. His ruddy cheeks had red splotches, but he didn't seem to be sick. Sandy hair too short for a ponytail fell over his forehead.

The third boy was younger. He was thin with a neat ponytail and eyes that danced. He took in every part of Johnny in a strange way that made Johnny uncomfortable.

"Yes," said Johnny, not sure which of them had asked. "I'm Johnny Adams."

"Great to meet you. I'm Deane," said the rounder one. "This is Vernon," pointing at the tall one. "And the little skinny here is Gus."

"I'm not skinny," said Gus.

"You are skinny," said Deane.

"Everyone is skinny compared to you," said Gus.

Deane ignored Gus. "Johnny, the captain said to

find you and then find Mr. Griffin so he can show us what to do."

But Mr. Griffin found them first. "You look like you're feeling better than last night, Johnny. You've met Vernon, Deane and Gus. Are you ready to learn the ship?"

"Yes, sir," said Johnny.

"Say, 'aye,' instead of 'yes.' It carries better on the wind. And I'm not a 'sir.' Just a mister."

"Aye, Mr. Griffin," said Johnny.

"Now, boys, we're in dangerous waters," said Mr. Griffin with twinkling eyes. "Every able-bodied man or boy must be ready to help in a fight. Are you ready?"

"Aye," said Johnny.

"Aye," said Deane.

"Aye," said Gus.

They all turned to Vernon.

He yawned and stretched his arms wide. "Mr. Griffin, no man on this ship is more prepared to fight the British than I. The British have taken everything from me – my ships, my goods, my slaves. I have lost the most to the British which means I have the most reason to fight the British. In addition, I am well versed in the art of war. It's what I studied at Princetown."

"I've never heard war called an art," said Mr. Griffin suspiciously. "At least, there's no art in the fights I've seen. It's all smoke and crashing and blood."

19

"You cannot be expected to know what I mean," said Vernon. "But you are expected to know that my father is head of the American Navy. I have been with him in the war counsels. It is much more than smoke and crashing and blood. It is strategy. It is much larger and more important than these sailors or this ship."

"This ship," Mr. Griffin said in an even tone. "Is the only thing that will get you to France. Not 'strategy.' Only this ship. The captain of this ship has ordered all able-bodied boys to be ready. Which means I will test you, and you will do the test. Follow me."

Vernon huffed and pretended to yawn again, but followed. Johnny, Deane and Gus walked eagerly after Mr. Griffin.

Deane whispered to Johnny, "Bad luck I share a cabin with Vernon. He likes to order me around. But I think he's afraid of my skin sores. Maybe it's bad luck for him rather than me. I don't know. But don't worry. It's not contagious. The sores, I mean, not luck. Maybe luck's contagious. I don't know. But don't worry about the sores."

They followed Mr. Griffin past the main mast. It jutted high from the middle of the ship and had four sails. Off the front was the foremast, with a long spar going forward. Below it was a high platform.

"That platform at the front is the forecastle," said Deane. "Doesn't look anything like a castle. I don't know why they call it a forecastle. But there's a cannon up there. So maybe that's why it's called a castle. Not one of the big cannons, though. The big cannons are on the sides."

At the stairs to the forecastle, Mr. Griffin went up first, then Gus. Deane went next, struggling to climb. Johnny waited and leapt up behind him. Vernon followed slowly.

Mr. Griffin saw something wrong in the main sail and went back to the quarterdeck to yell at some sailors. Gus followed him. Vernon ignored Johnny and Deane and pulled out a spyglass to look at the sea.

Alone with Deane, Johnny asked him, "Are you here by yourself?"

Deane nodded. "My father's in France. I'm going to be with him. My uncle and aunt had me for the last couple of years, but they got tired of waiting for my father to come back. They decided to send me to him. Better for me. They kept me cooped up. But I didn't know you and your father were going to be here. That's amazing! Your father is famous! What's it like to live with a famous father?"

Johnny shrugged. "He's not there, most of the time. Usually, he's in Philadelphia or Boston. But more often, Philadelphia. What's your father doing in France?"

Deane looked sideways at Johnny. "It's a secret. I'm not supposed to know, but I do. I heard him tell my uncle."

"What secret?" asked Johnny.

21

Mr. Griffin interrupted. "Mr. Deane, you'll climb first. Grab the first spar and climb the foremast. Stay over the ship and don't go too high."

"Why are we doing this, Mr. Griffin?" interrupted Vernon. "Why on earth are we to climb a mast?"

"It's a test, Mr. Vernon," answered Mr. Griffin. "In a sea battle or any other battle, you lose men, as you with all your expertise in the art of war should know. When you lose men, you need other men to replace them. Sometimes, boys. Boys who can climb a mast and be a lookout."

"I'm not a —" started Vernon.

Mr. Griffin interrupted him. "Are you ready, Mr. Deane?"

"Aye, aye," said Deane with a grin.

"Stay over the ship and don't go too high," said Mr. Griffin.

"Aye, aye," said Deane again.

Going too high wasn't a problem for Deane. He grabbed the first spar but couldn't lift himself any higher. Johnny went to help, but Mr. Griffin held him back.

"If he can't get up on his own, he won't be able to get down on his own," said Mr. Griffin quietly. Loudly, he said, "That's all right, Mr. Deane. We'll find another job for you. Gus, your turn."

Gus grabbed the spar and tried to pull himself up. His arms were too weak, so he lifted his legs and wrapped them around the spar. Twisting sideways, he rolled over and sat on the spar.

"Well done, Gus," said Mr. Griffin. "Take this rope and tie it to the spar. Tie the other end around your waist for safety."

Mr. Griffin tossed the rope. Gus grabbed it and wrapped it around the spar. But his arms were too short. Laying on the spar, he couldn't tie them together.

"That's good for now, Gus," said Mr. Griffin. "Come down and we'll see what Johnny can do."

Gus started to protest, but Mr. Griffin said, "Down quickly, Gus!"

Johnny grabbed the spar and started to pull himself up, but Mr. Griffin stopped him.

He pointed at Johnny's scarred finger. "Can you grip with that, Johnny?"

Johnny opened and closed his finger. "It's perfectly fine. Just scarred." He put his hand around the rope and pulled. "See?"

Mr. Griffin took Johnny's hand and looked at the finger. "With all those scars, it's amazing you can move it at all."

"It was almost amputated, but Dr. Warren fixed it," said Johnny.

"Dr. Warren of Boston? Of Bunker Hill?" asked Mr. Griffin.

Johnny nodded. "His son Joey is my friend."

"Such a loss. Such a sad loss." Mr. Griffin shook his head. "Let's put what he saved to work. Grab the first spar and pull yourself up. Tie one end of the rope around the spar. The other end around your waist."

Johnny rose and tied himself quickly. He balanced like he did when he climbed trees in Braintree. The spar bent like a tree branch in a storm. It swayed as the ship cut through the waves.

Suddenly, the sick feeling returned to Johnny's throat. He took a deep breath, and it went away. "Now what, Mr. Griffin?" asked Johnny.

"Go to the foremast and find the grips. Climb to the bottom of the sail above. And always keep three touches. Two feet and one arm. Two arms and one foot. Always three touches. Move only one arm or foot at a time."

Johnny climbed. He reached the bottom of the sail and looked down.

The ship moved beneath him. Johnny held on and pulled the rope on his waist tighter.

"I'm here. Now what?" asked Johnny.

"Come down. I've seen what you can do," said Mr. Griffin. "We'll let Mr. Vernon –"

Mr. Griffin's words were cut off by a ripping sound. Johnny looked up and saw a torn piece of canvas. Some of it was bunched and caught under another rope. With too much tension on it, the canvas tore a little more with each dip and rise through the sea.

Johnny saw that he could fix it. If he pulled the canvas free, the tearing would stop.

Mr. Griffin saw what Johnny was thinking. "It's too far, Johnny. Come back down. I'll call a sailor."

The sail tore again.

"I'll get it. I just need to pull the canvas." said Johnny.

"All right," said Mr. Griffin. "Loop your rope around that hook on the spar and be quick about it!"

Johnny looped the rope around the hook. He wrapped his legs around the beam like Gus had done. He hung underneath and inched out along the spar. Spray coated his back. He was going out over the sea. His heart beat faster. He looked down and salty water hit his face.

"Can you reach it, Johnny?" called Mr. Griffin.

"Aye," said Johnny. He reached the end of the wet spar. He put a hand toward the canvas. He gripped the corner and pulled.

It didn't budge.

The ship rose on a swell. High above the sea, the sail caught the wind. The canvas snapped against Johnny's hand.

Johnny lost his grip. His other hand slipped off the spar.

He swung upside down by his feet. "Three touches, Johnny!" yelled Mr. Griffin as the rope on Johnny's waist pulled taut.

"Aye!" said Johnny. Johnny tightened his knees and flexed his stomach and swung back to the beam. He caught his breath and looked again at the sail.

"Better come down, Johnny!" shouted Mr. Griffin.

"I can do it!" answered Johnny. He edged out further and waited for the ship's bow to dip.

Without the wind, the sail slackened.

Johnny grabbed a fistful of canvas.

With all his strength, Johnny pulled.

The sail came free.

"All right, then, Johnny!" said Mr. Griffin with relief.

Johnny inched back along the beam. He shimmied down the foremast and dropped to the forecastle.

"Well done, Johnny!" said Deane.

"Well done, Johnny," said Gus, mocking Deane.

Vernon ignored them. He stared through his spyglass at the sea.

"Aye, Johnny," said Mr. Griffin. "Well done but I don't think we'll do that again soon."

"Someone had to do it," shrugged Johnny.

"Aye. Not bad for a boy with a scarred hand," said Mr. Griffin.

As Johnny untied himself from the safety rope, he saw his fingers were shaking. He held them out in front of him. He couldn't stop the shaking, so he folded them together. He opened them again, and they shook some more.

A shout came from the main mast. It was a voice Johnny thought he recognized. Was it the voice from the night before? The voice who talked about the secret plans?

Then another voice joined in. And many others. Finally, Johnny made out what they were saying.

"Three ships to the north!"

Vernon shouted back, "Where? I don't see them!"

Mr. Griffin ignored Vernon and shouted back, "What flags?"

"British flags, Mr. Griffin!"

"Ring the bell!" ordered Mr. Griffin.

Chapter Three

At the sound of the bell, sailors streamed from the hatches.

They climbed into the masts and looked to the southeast.

Johnny squinted, but he couldn't see any ships anywhere. He followed Mr. Griffin to the stern of the ship. Gus ran ahead, ducked into a cabin and emerged by the wheel.

There was Captain Tucker waiting for the spyglass that Gus handed him.

It was the first time Johnny had seen the captain in daylight.

When they met at Cousin Norton's house by the shore the previous day, it had already been dark. The captain was sitting slumped over the kitchen table, his face lit by candlelight. His dark brow hung over sunken eyes, and he was in a sour mood.

Then Norton's wife Adelia had surprised them, and the captain nearly shot her.

It had started with a rustle in the back room. Then a slammed door.

In a flash, Captain Tucker's pistol was in his hand.

"No – no, put that away," said Norton, a sick look on his face. "It's just my wife."

Adelia ghosted in a nightdress. Her hair was flying.

She focused wild eyes on Johnny's father.

"John. And Johnny boy. You are welcome here. And you, Captain."

"Thank you, Adelia, for your hospitality," replied Johnny's father. "But there is no need –"

"John Adams," interrupted Adelia. "Do not go on Captain Tucker's ship this night."

Johnny saw his father's eyes narrow. "Oh? Why is that?"

"An ill wind is brewing," said Adelia. "The heavens frown. The clouds roll. The waves roar upon the beach. You are embarking on this journey under ill omens!"

A chill went down Johnny's spine. She sounded like a soothsayer from the Greek myths. Cassandra. The predictor of evil.

Was this a curse?

Johnny's father was unimpressed. "We are taking every precaution, Adelia. I am not enough of a Roman to believe in omens. We trust in more powerful forces than the weather."

Adelia fell forward like she'd been struck. Norton caught her just above the floor. Johnny tried to help, but Norton waved him away. "I have her," he said as he carried her back to her room.

Captain Tucker's brow somehow grew darker. "Mr. Adams, I myself have no belief in soothsaying or such, but I'll ask you and Johnny to not speak of this to any sailors. They put much weight on the stars and such. They don't even like women aboard. They think

29

they bring bad luck."

"Of course," said Johnny's father.

The captain turned to Johnny. "Yes, Captain," Johnny said quickly.

The captain nodded and went back to his drink.

Aboard the ship, Captain Tucker was very different.

Looking through his spyglass, he was in command. He had men's lives in his hands.

He had authority.

"Well done, Mr. Welch," said Captain Tucker to the helmsman. "Putting the Britishers on our stern. Keep our heading. Gus, please ask Mr. Adams to join me."

"I can get him," said Johnny, turning to go.

"No, Johnny, your young eyes can be useful here," said Captain Tucker, offering his spyglass. "How many guns do you see on the biggest ship?"

Johnny turned the focus on the spyglass. The three ships looked no bigger. "Twist the other way," instructed the captain.

A mighty sailing ship filled the view.

"Sixteen along the side, Captain," said Johnny. "Does that mean it's a man-of-war?"

"Aye, it does," said the captain solemnly. "The other two ships are also fit for battle. But it's strange for them to be in these waters. They should be further south this time of year. It's as if they were looking for us."

Vernon had his own spyglass up. Eagerly, he

asked, "Will we fight them?"

"That's a question I'll discuss with Mr. Adams," said Captain Tucker. "Either way, we'll watch them first. We'll make some turns and judge their seamanship. We'll learn how to beat them, if it comes to that."

Lieutenant Jamison arrived with five Marines, muskets loaded. "Into the masts, Captain?"

"Hold here, Lieutenant, until I discuss with Mr. Adams," said the captain. "But be ready."

Johnny's father arrived at the stern. Johnny could see he had dressed quickly, but neatly. His shoes were buckled. His shirt was straight. His coat was buttoned to the top.

"Mr. Adams," said the captain. "We seem to have been found by Britishers, which requires some conversation, if you will join me."

"Should we have Dr. Noel's counsel?" asked Johnny's father.

"No," said Captain Tucker. "I know what he'll say."

Johnny started to follow but was tugged back by Deane. "What's happening, Johnny? Will there be a fight?"

"I'm trying to listen," answered Johnny, pulling away.

"There had best be a fight," said Vernon icily. "My father says any chance to engage the British should be taken. The British won't respect us if we run. Especially not in our own waters."

"They have thirty-two guns on one ship against our twenty-four guns. Plus, two more ships," Gus said.

Vernon laughed. "If the captain has the right qualities, guns shouldn't matter. Battles are won by the most courageous, the most indefatigable. Not by the ship with the most guns."

"The most inde-what?" asked Deane.

"Indefatigable," repeated Vernon. "Those who do not get tired."

"What about the smartest?" teased Gus. "Don't the smartest win battles?"

"Of course, but the –" Vernon was interrupted by a shout from the Captain.

"Mr. Griffin, raise every inch of canvas. Mr. Welch, hold the wheel for maximum speed. Keep the bearing as south as you can. Mr. Jamison, your Marines are some hours away from being needed, but have them ready."

"Aye, aye," cascaded through the officers.

The sailors didn't wait for the orders to be repeated. They leaped to work. They ferried canvas into the masts. They unfurled all the sails. They tightened the ropes. Johnny's father took the Captain's spyglass to the stern.

Vernon was aghast. "You will run, Captain?"

"Aye, for now," said the captain. "We will test their speed and turns."

Vernon flashed red with anger. "Has not my father, Commissioner of the Naval Board, ordered you to take and destroy any Britishers you see?"

"There are other things in play, Mr. Vernon."

"But my father's orders –" started Vernon.

"Your father's orders?" interrupted Captain Tucker, his face dark again like at Cousin Norton's house. "Your father gave me orders, aye. He also made me captain. Which means whether to run or fight is done as I see it. There are bigger things in play than a boy's romantic desire for battle."

"It's cowardly to run from a fight," said Vernon, puffing out his chest.

Captain Tucker put a finger against Vernon's puffed out chest. "You, boy, have a child's view of war. I'll stand for some questions. But not on my courage. Not by a boy who's never been in a fight!"

Vernon's chest deflated. He opened his mouth, but no words came out. He turned and stormed off.

Gus laughed.

Captain Tucker turned to Gus and frowned. "Keep an eye on him, Gus. Tell me if – if he's up to no good."

"Aye, aye, Captain," said Gus with a smile.

Johnny's father returned from the stern. "Captain, how soon could they catch us?"

"Not soon, Mr. Adams," answered the Captain. "The *Boston* is a quick ship. We're not heavily loaded. We'll run ahead of them for some time. At least a day."

"Good," said Johnny's father. "Johnny, let's get below. I need your help on a chemical message."

Chapter Four

"This message was aboard when we arrived last night," said Johnny's father. "Hold the glass bowl steady. I'll mix the chemicals. The chemicals must go on the paper quickly for it to work."

Johnny's father took two vials of liquid from a bag. Johnny held the bowl carefully on the tilting desk. His father dumped the vials into the bowl and mixed them.

"What is it?" asked Johnny.

Johnny's father ignored the question and took out a small brush. "Now, hold the paper while I apply the liquid."

On the paper was handwriting. It said something about the weather in Philadelphia. "Who's it from?"

"Mr. Jay," said Johnny's father. "Hold the paper still."

Johnny's father dropped the brush on the paper and swept the liquid across. "You're going to smudge the writing, Pappa," said Johnny.

"It's not this writing I'm trying to read," said Johnny's father.

Something new appeared. Vertical lines first, then horizontal connectors.

A secret message?

"Hold the paper still, Johnny," said Johnny's father again.

"What does it say?"

Johnny's father took the paper and read it. "There are names. It looks like instructions for meetings in France. But I can't read it. Hold the corners again."

Johnny's father swept the wet brush across the paper.

Nothing more appeared.

Johnny's father sighed. "Typical of secret things. They never work as planned."

"Can you put more liquid on it?" asked Johnny.

"The problem's not with our liquid. Mr. Jay didn't have the right mixture when he wrote it. That's why it's unreadable." Johnny's father held the paper over the candle. It caught flame.

"Useless," sighed Johnny's father. "Now I don't know whom they want me to meet in France."

"Pappa, are these secret plans? Plans that a spy would want to steal?"

"A spy? Why? Where did you get that idea?"

"I heard some sailors talking last night. One said he was working for Lord West. The other was looking for secret plans."

"I've never heard of a Lord West. And secret plans? This was the only secret plan I had, and it's unreadable." Johnny's father laughed. "If there are spies, they're wasting their time. Everybody knows why I'm going to France. We need French ships to break the British blockade on our coast. Everybody knows that's why Dr. Franklin is France. Everybody knows that's why I'm going to France. Even the British."

"But there was some secret," said Johnny. "Because Mr. Jay wrote it with chemicals."

"And now it's a secret from me, since Mr. Jay didn't mix his chemicals correctly. Useless!" Johnny's father shook his head. "This war won't be won with secrets, Johnny. It will be won the way wars are always won: by being on the side of justice. We will bring the truth to the King of France. We will tell him of British injustices, and he cannot help but support our cause."

Johnny wondered if there was something else. Some other secret plan. The sailors hadn't said anything about Johnny's father. But they had talked about a box. And the captain's cabin boy. Gus?

"Could there be something else secret?" asked Johnny. "A secret box?"

"Forget secrets, Johnny. Dr. Franklin and Dr. Noel and the Committee think secrets are important. They think secrets will win us French support. But they are wrong. Secrets only give an advantage in the short term. More often, they get in the way. Like this secret writing Mr. Jay sent me."

"Who is Dr. Noel? Who is the Committee?" asked Johnny.

Johnny's father sighed. "The Committee is best ignored. As for Dr. Noel, you will meet him soon. Perhaps tonight at the captain's table. If you are fortunate, he will tutor you in French. Now, I must write to the newspapers. There are many like our neighbor Mr. Hanford who still need convincing. Do you have your Plutarch to read?"

With that, Johnny's father turned to his desk. He took out a fresh sheet of paper, dipped his quill and started writing.

Johnny pulled out his English Plutarch and climbed into his hammock. He looked at the pages, but the words blurred.

Secrets and chemical messages and committees? And his father said they were best ignored?

Before he left home, his mother told him he was entering the world in which he should live.

His father's world.

But what was it? A world of Lords and secrets and chasing ships?

When his mother told Johnny he would go with his father to France, he had been worried about the farm. He had been worried about who would do the work that he had done. They had supplies for the rest of the winter, but what about planting season? And harvest? And care of the animals in every season? How would his mother and Nabby and little brothers do it all?

He was glad to be with his father, but was it right to leave? Should he have tried harder to stay home?

The night Johnny left home, he had asked his mother again.

"Mamma, how can you work the farm without

me?"

His mother answered quickly, "Nabby will do more. I will do more. Charley and Tommy are getting old enough to work. We will be fine."

"Tommy can't even carry water without spilling!" Johnny had said.

"Not so long ago, you couldn't, either," she had said. "He will learn."

"But when spring comes, there's –"

"Johnny, we need you," Johnny's mother said with misty eyes. "And when I think about the dangers ahead of you, my heart sinks. The British ships. The winter storms. And in France – I don't want to think about that. The conspiracies. The Germans and Austrians and Russians with their wars . . . But it comes to this: Every boy must someday leave his mother. That day is here for you. You are entering the world in which you must live. Angels guard and protect thee, and may a safe return ere long bless thee."

With that, she straightened Johnny's coat. She fixed his collar. She pushed the hair off his forehead. "Don't forget to brush your teeth" were her last words before they left for Cousin Norton's.

And then they had met Captain Tucker. And taken the skiff to the *Boston*. And Johnny's stomach had revolted. Which led him to the barrel by the rail. Where he heard two sailors talking about secret plans. And a strongbox.

Now he remembered.

The sailor said "strongbox" in a strange way. He said the last sound in a guttural way. Like he was swallowing it and spitting it out. Not like an American. Or an Englishman. Like a German?

The ship's bell rang for dinner.

Johnny's father blotted his quill and stood up.

"Time for the captain's table, Johnny. Perhaps you'll meet Dr. Noel."

Chapter Five

The glow of the British ships filled the window at the back of the Captain's cabin.

Hands planted on the captain's desk, Vernon was staring at them. His face was clouded by a nasty, malevolent look. His body was coiled up like he was ready to spring through the window at the British ships.

At the front of the cabin was the captain and the ship's officers, swords swaying at their waists. Johnny's father joined them. Gus had his back to Vernon, arranging a box of silver forks and knives. The cook and his assistant held ready a stack of plates near the door. Candles glimmered on the table, their light reflected in brass instruments hanging between books on both walls. There was no one else in the room. No one who could be a French doctor. No Dr. Noel.

Deane burst through the door and sided up to Johnny. "What did I miss?" he asked with a grin.

"Nothing," said Johnny.

"Nothing?" said Deane, still grinning.

Johnny raised an eyebrow. "What's making you so happy?"

"I don't know. I'm sorry. I'm just happy – I'm just

happy to be here. Happy to be on this ship. Happy to be going to see my father. Happy to be out of my uncle's house! How's the bread?"

"I don't know," said Johnny.

"Let's find out," whispered Deane.

Deane put his hands behind his back. He casually backed up to the table. He reached back and felt around until he found a piece of bread. He tore a piece off and moved it toward his mouth.

A hand grabbed his wrist. Another hand grabbed the bread from Deane's hand.

"Excuse me, gentlemen," said Gus from the side. "If you would take your seats."

"What the –" said Deane. "Give it back!"

"It's the captain's until it's served. As his guest, you should refrain until served."

Deane plopped down and muttered, "What's wrong with that boy? It's just bread."

The captain turned to the group and said, "If you would please take your seats, gentlemen."

Johnny sat next to Deane as the door came open again.

A large man filled the doorway. His head nearly reached the ceiling. His shoulders were bunched with knotty muscle. Across his forehead was combed long hair. His wide lips were set in a line. He scanned the room quickly and sat in the chair opposite the captain. He put his hands on the table, and Johnny saw they were nicked with white lines of scars.

"Welcome, Dr. Noel!" said the captain. "Gus,

another place setting, please!"

Gus pulled a key from a string around his neck and used it to open a metal box against the wall. He took out a silver knife and fork and placed it in front of Dr. Noel.

"Let us pray," said the captain.

Everyone bowed their heads, but Johnny's mind was on what Gus had just done.

Was that the strongbox? The strongbox the sailors had talked about? If that was the strongbox, that's where the secret plans were. They had to be.

The captain prayed for the ship's safety and everyone said, "Amen." The cook deposited two roasted chickens on the table. On pewter plates came a stack of cooked potatoes, a pile of green string beans and rice. Gus filled Johnny and Deane's glasses with weak cider. Before he could fill Vernon's glass, Vernon put his hand over it.

"Wine for me, boy," said Vernon. At a nod from Captain Tucker, Gus gave Vernon wine.

Dr. Noel took small portions as each plate came by, letting out a sigh at each.

The captain laughed. "Dr. Noel, I apologize for our practical food. It is meant for fuel rather than pleasure."

"It is possible for both," Dr. Noel answered gruffly.

The captain laughed loudly. If there was a joke, Johnny didn't get it.

The captain said, "Doctor, have you heard the

story about the Frenchman with a cure for fleas?"

"There is no cure for fleas," answered Dr. Noel.

"Ah, but a Frenchman in London found one. It was a powder. When he advertised it, Londoners flocked to buy it. One lady asked how to use it." Captain Tucker pursed his lips and spoke with a French accent '*Madame*,' said the Frenchman. 'You must catch the flea and squeeze him between the fingers until the mouth is open. Then you must put the powder in his mouth. Then he will never bite you again.' The London lady was surprised. 'But,' she said, 'if I can catch the flea, then I can kill the flea myself.' The Frenchman threw up his hands and said, 'Well, you should do that, then!'"

The captain and the officers roared with laughter. Dr. Noel's eyebrows narrowed. He dropped another layer of salt on his food.

Deane turned to Johnny. "I don't understand. Is that supposed to be funny?"

Johnny shrugged, and Deane spooned a large helping of potatoes into his mouth.

Dr. Noel looked at Deane. "Monsieur Deane, it is?"

With his cheeks stuffed with potatoes, Deane could only answer, "Ooof?"

"You are Mr. Deane, yes?" asked Dr. Noel again.

Deane swallowed, but his cheeks were still half-full. "Esss"

"What are you doing for your rickets, Monsieur Deane?"

Deane took a drink of cider to wash down the potatoes, and tried to answer Dr. Noel's question at the same time. "I don't –" A mix of wet potatoes escaped and dribbled down his shirt. "Sorry." Deane dabbed with his handkerchief and smeared the potatoes on his shirt. "I don't have rickets."

Dr. Noel reached across Johnny and grabbed Deane's hand. He held it in the air.

"What are you doing?" asked Deane, trying to pull away.

Deane's sleeve fell down, exposing his wrist. It was wide where it should have been narrow.

"You have rickets. It is why your wrist is wide. It is why you have sores."

"No – my uncle says – it was a childhood disease. A sickness of sores."

"Did your uncle keep you inside all day. Out of the sun?"

Deane nodded. "Yes. So it wouldn't get worse."

"You are very fortunate to be gone from there," said Dr. Noel. "When the weather is better, you will see," said Dr. Noel.

"What does that mean? The weather?" asked Deane.

Dr. Noel ignored Deane and turned to Vernon. "You are the Vernon boy, yes?"

"Good sir," answered Vernon, his hawk nose in the air. "I would very much appreciate if you do not refer to me as a 'boy'."

"Would you like to learn French before arriving in

France?" asked Dr. Noel.

"I know Greek and Latin and Aramaic and have a talent for languages. I expect no trouble learning French."

"Well, then," said Dr. Noel with a nod. "You have no need of me."

"Thank you, I do not," said Vernon.

Dr. Noel looked Johnny over from fingertips to face to hair, then looked in Johnny's eyes and nodded. "Your first French lesson is tomorrow morning."

It wasn't a question. It was an order.

"Can I come?" asked Deane eagerly.

Dr. Noel grimaced at Deane's potato-smeared shirt.

Johnny said, "It will help me to have someone to practice with, Dr. Noel. Can you teach us both?"

Dr. Noel sighed. "You must be clean in my cabin, Mr. Deane. No food, *compris*?"

"Complete?" asked Deane. "What's complete?"

"*Compris*," repeated Dr. Noel. "It means, 'understood.' Is it understood? No food."

"Oh, yes," said Deane. "Understood."

At the end of dinner, Gus and the cook's assistant cleared the plates. Dr. Noel, Johnny's father, the captain and his officers took a yellowish drink to the broad window. Vernon insisted on joining them, leaving Johnny and Deane alone at the table.

"Did you see the strongbox?" asked Johnny.

"Where they keep the silver?" asked Deane. "Wait – Do you think it's the strongbox you heard the spy talking about?"

"It could be," said Johnny. "If so, Gus is in danger. We should tell him."

"Tell him what? That you heard a spy who wanted the key to the strongbox?"

"Yes," said Johnny.

"All right," said Deane with a shrug. "Gus, over here."

Gus was stacking the last of the plates. He looked over with a frown. "What do you want? More bread?"

"Do you have any?" asked Deane. Then he shook it off. "No, not bread. We wanted to ask you about the strongbox."

"What about it?" asked Gus suspiciously.

Johnny answered, "Who else has a key? Is it just you?"

"My – the captain has one, too," said Gus. "Why do you want to know?"

Johnny looked sideways at Deane. "We – I think you might be in danger. I heard a sailor, maybe a spy, say he wants a secret from the strongbox."

Gus laughed. "There's no secret in the strongbox. But there is silver. And a little gold. Maybe that's what the sailor wanted." Gus grew serious. "Did he say how he planned to get it?"

"No," answered Johnny. "But if it's only you and the captain who have a key, he's probably coming after you."

Suddenly there was a shout from the window.

It was Vernon. He pointed and yelled at the British

ships. Then he cursed them. Then he cursed King George. He counted on his fingers all that the British had taken from his family. It was almost the same speech as before. Ships. Goods. Slaves.

"That's enough, Mr. Vernon," said the captain. "We've all lost a lot to the British."

"Not as much – not as much as I have," slurred Vernon. "I've lost as much – more than much. A lot . . ."

"Mr. Deane," said the captain. "Would you help Mr. Vernon back to his cabin?"

Deane got up and grabbed Vernon's arm. "Let's go, Vernon."

Vernon pulled his arm away. "Do not touch me with your nasty sores."

The cook's assistant came and loomed over Vernon.

"All right. All right. I'll go," slurred Vernon.

Deane and the cook's assistant took Vernon back to his cabin.

When they were gone, Dr. Noel went to the door and blocked it.

He turned to the officers, said, "Remember gentlemen, there is a British spy aboard. If you have any knowledge or hint of who it might be, please let me know immediately."

Before Johnny could speak, Dr. Noel was gone. Johnny was stunned.

Dr. Noel knew there was a British spy aboard?

The ship's officers knew there was a British spy

aboard?

Everyone knew?

Before Johnny could follow Dr. Noel, his father put an arm around his shoulder.

"Enough conversation, Johnny. Back to the quill and paper for me. That means back to the books for you. Do we have enough candles?"

Chapter Six

When Johnny got up the next morning, his stomach rolled less than the day before. And when it rolled, it rolled with the ship. Up and down a little. Side to side. It felt natural. Natural enough to wonder how to talk to Dr. Noel about the spy.

Dr. Noel said at dinner he would teach Johnny French. But he hadn't said when. Or where.

Johnny decided to find Dr. Noel and ask. The ship wasn't that big. It shouldn't take long.

Johnny pulled on his boots and found his feet balancing before the floor moved. He grabbed the water pail. Climbing through the hatch, he stood on the quarterdeck and breathed the morning air.

The British ships were in the distance. Smaller than they had been in the Captain's window.

The sailors moved around in darting paths. Quicker than they had yesterday. More carefully, too. They kept one eye on the British ships. Like the British might suddenly jump closer. A few ate their morning meal next to the rail. A bite, then a look up. Like squirrels with nuts.

Clouds moved as fast as the ship, which made them seem not to move at all. There was no longer land beyond the green-gray sea. Seagulls trailed after the ship, diving into the ship's wake and coming up with struggling fish.

Johnny wondered where to look for Dr. Noel. By the captain's cabin? Beneath it? Or lower in the ship. Johnny thought that was where the sailors had their bunks. But he hadn't been there yet. Then Johnny realized Dr. Noel's cabin wouldn't be there. He must be where Johnny and his father were. There were four doors in the companion cabin hallway. Johnny and his father had one. Vernon and Deane had another. That left two doors. One of which was Dr. Noel's. Should he knock on both?

But if he found him, what would he say?

"Good morning, Johnny," said a chipper Deane, interrupting Johnny's thoughts. "Have you had food?"

"No," said Johnny.

"Come on, then," said Deane. "I'll show you where to get it. If the sailors will let us through."

Johnny started to object, but Deane had already squeezed his wide body down the main hatch.

Johnny followed and found himself in a low, wide area. The ceiling was only a foot over Johnny's head and held up by wide timbers. A few steps from the stairs was a room with a thick door secured by a hefty padlock.

"That's the gunpowder room," said Deane. "They keep the cannonballs there, too. You think the captain would let us play with one?"

"Probably not," said Johnny.

"Probably not," agreed Deane.

Beyond the gunpowder room were stacked bags, crates and barrels with a narrow pathway through them. In the dim light, Johnny couldn't see how far it went. Behind him came the sounds of animals. Chickens clucked, pigs snorted, and a cow lowed.

Deane waved Johnny toward the animal sounds. "The kitchen is this way. Food should be ready, but we can also get some eggs if the cook doesn't catch us."

Through the open kitchen door were six bench tables with men crowded around. Past a line of sailors Johnny saw the cook and cook's assistant in front of a stone hearth. A chimney pulled smoke into the low ceiling, but not all of it went up. The dank smoke, the nasty animal smells and the savory scent of cooked foods combined into a stench worse than anything Johnny had ever smelled on land.

Johnny held his nose and Deane laughed. "If you think it smells bad now, wait til we go lower. The sailors smell even worse than the food they eat."

Deane and Johnny joined the line of sailors. As they got closer, Johnny saw two enormous pots resting on holes in the hearth. Inside, meats of a strange color were boiling. Behind them were ovens cast from iron, with doors the cook and his assistant opened with towels. They pulled out bread and tore it and put it on the sailors' plates. Then a piece of meat from the boiling pots went on each plate and the sailors shuffled to their tables.

When Deane and Johnny got to the front of the

line, the cook's assistant didn't look up until he saw they didn't have plates. "Now, boys, what's this? Too hungry to wait for a meal in your cabin?"

"I'm trying to get some bread for Johnny," said Deane quickly. "His stomach isn't quite right. Bread should help."

The cook's assistant looked at Johnny and handed Deane a loaf of bread. "All right. Here you are boys."

Deane took it. "Thank you. Do you have any butter?"

The cook's assistant laughed. "You'll need a better story for butter, boy. It's in short supply on a ship. Only when the captain wants it. Now be gone! Lots more mouths to feed."

Outside the kitchen, Deane tore the bread in half. "You can choose which half, Johnny."

Johnny's stomach rumbled at the offer. "No thanks, Deane. You can have both."

Deane smiled. "Thanks! The salted beef is stacked around that corner, if you want some. There's a back way to the chickens, too, if you want eggs."

Johnny shook his head. "I'm fine."

"Are you fine enough to go lower? The smell is worse, but I heard there's a sailor with a rubber ball. I want to see if he'll trade something for it."

Johnny shrugged. "All right. Let's go."

Deane led down another set of stairs. At the bottom, a lit candle showed sailors crammed in cots. There were provisions stacked in every corner. Crates stood from floor to ceiling.

The air was damp, and the smell was terrible. An oily sick kind of smell. The sailors didn't seem to mind. Maybe they were used to it. There were no portholes. They were below the water line.

"Hello there, boys," said a sailor with bushy black sideburns. "What brings you down so low? Britishers closing in?"

"No," said Deane. "They're still in the distance. I – I heard one of you might have a rubber ball to trade."

All eyes turned toward Deane and Johnny. The black sideburned sailor slipped out of his cot and said, "I think we could find you a rubber ball, boy. What do you have to trade?"

"I don't know. What do you need?"

All eyes looked Deane up and down. "Are those silver buckles on your shoes?"

"Yes," said Deane. "But they're worth more than a rubber ball."

"Aye," said the sailor. "I agree. Trading for it wouldn't be fair. But gambling would be. Do you know the game of Hazard? I'll give you three chances to win a ball. To get a buckle, I'd have to win all three. You'd only need to win one. Three to one odds. That would be fair, wouldn't it?"

The other sailors nodded and murmured. "Fair." "Yes, fair." "Three chances against one would be more than fair."

"But I don't know how to play Hallard," said Deane. "Was it Hallard?"

"Hazard," said the sailor. "No problem. It's very

53

simple. You roll the dice. We'll teach you."

Deane looked at Johnny.

Johnny asked the sailor, "How does it work?"

"We use two six-sided dice," said the sailor. "You choose a number between 5 and 9. The number you choose is called your 'main.' If you roll your main on the first try, you win. If you roll an 11 or 12, you might win, depending on your main. If you roll a 2 or a 3, you lose. If you roll a number between 5 and 9 that's not your main, you roll again. On the second roll —"

"That's really complicated," said Deane.

"I think I understand," said Johnny. "What happens on the second roll?"

"On the second roll, none of the numbers matter except what you got on the first roll and your main. Except winning and losing is reversed. If you roll the same number again from your first roll, you win. If you roll your main on the second roll, you lose. You keep rolling until you win or lose."

"Aren't the best odds with 7 as your main?" asked Johnny.

The circle of sailors nodded.

"If you choose 7, aren't your odds about 50/50?" asked Johnny.

The circle of sailors nodded again.

"And you're giving Deane three chances to win?" asked Johnny.

"Yes," said the sailor. "Three chances to win."

Johnny shrugged. "It seems like a good bet, Deane,

if you choose a 7 as your main."

"All right," said Deane. "I'll take 7 for the main. Where are the dice?"

A whoop went up from the circle of sailors.

"Spread back, men. Let the boy have space to roll!"

Deane took the dice. He shook them in his hand and threw them.

They bounced off a sailor's boot and landed.

"A 2 and a 1!" said the sailor. "That makes 3. Bad luck, boy. You lose. But you've got two more chances."

Johnny's stomach rumbled. It was loud enough for Deane to hear it.

"I need fresh air," said Johnny. "Quick."

Deane nodded. "I'll win the ball and find you later."

Johnny climbed back up the stairs. In the main hold, the animal smells brought Johnny nausea again. He caught himself against the gunpowder room and rushed to a porthole. He put his face into the fresh air and fought the urge to vomit.

Suddenly he missed home. Where everything was solid. Where nothing swayed. Where there was always fresh air.

Johnny sat on a crate and put his head between his legs. He tried to stay as still as possible.

The ship went through a smooth patch of sea. Everything went quiet, and Johnny heard a strange sound in the far corner of the hold.

It was a faint scratching, but it was away from where the animals were. An escaped animal? Or a rat? Johnny moved quietly through the crates and barrels. He stopped and listened. He heard the scratching again, this time with a whisper.

Was it the spy?

Searching for the secret plans?

Johnny put his back against a crate.

A familiar voice whispered, "Greetings, Josephine. How are you today?"

A girl? There's a girl aboard?

Johnny tiptoed closer and heard, "Come, sweet sleep, the friendless stranger, Woos thee to relieve his woes, Shield his head from every danger, Guard the wandering youth's repose."

A lullaby?

Johnny edged past the crate and looked with one eye.

Johnny gasped.

Chapter Seven

Gus was combing a doll's hair. And singing a lullaby.

Gus stopped at Johnny's gasp and was in his face in a flash. "What did you see?"

"I – I saw you combing a doll's hair," stammered Johnny. "And singing a lullaby."

Gus looked down. "Please don't tell. Father made me promise not to do girl things, but I need to talk to another girl, even if she's a doll."

Johnny was confused. "Girl? Father?"

Gus sighed. "Really, you aren't that smart. Your father is smart. Are you sure you weren't adopted?"

"What are you talking about?" asked Johnny.

"Simple," said Gus calmly. "I'm a girl."

"What?" asked Johnny, dumbfounded. "You can't be – you aren't – Girls can't be sailors!"

"That's why I'm dressed like this," said Gus. "My father said I could come if I worked and dressed like a cabin boy. He went to sea at my age. Girl or not, he said I could do the same."

"You're – a – girl?" was all Johnny could say.

"Thanks for catching up. Augusta is my real name. Nice to meet you." She offered her hand to shake Johnny's hand.

Johnny took it. Before he could react, Augusta had pulled him off balance, twisted him around and had her arm around his throat.

"Now, Johnny, my father would be in trouble if the crew finds out. You won't tell, will you?"

Johnny tried to nod, but it was impossible with her arm around his throat.

"Can you keep it a secret?"

"Yes," croaked Johnny. "Who else knows?"

"Mr. Griffin, but no one else."

"Why can't the sailors know?"

"They think girls are bad luck on a ship."

"Can you let me go?" asked Johnny.

"Do you promise not to tell anyone about me?" asked Augusta.

"I promise," said Johnny.

She released him. Johnny stood up and rubbed his neck. He was a little embarrassed to have been almost strangled by a girl. Then Johnny remembered something.

"That's why Mr. Griffin laughed when I said you were a spy," said Johnny. "He knew you were the captain's daughter. He knew you couldn't be a spy."

"Or maybe I am a spy," said Augusta. "Maybe I'm the perfect spy because I'm the captain's daughter."

That stopped Johnny. "Really? You're a spy?"

Augusta laughed. "No, you dolt. Are you sure you weren't adopted?"

"I wasn't adopted!"

"All right, all right," laughed Augusta. "You're not

adopted. What were you doing down here? Stealing eggs like Deane?"

"No – I was–" Johnny was interrupted by the bell on the quarterdeck.

"I've got to go," said Augusta. She rushed back to the half-open crate and stuffed her doll inside. Before she closed it, Johnny saw brass tubes gleaming inside.

"What's that in the crate?" asked Johnny.

"Ship's parts," said Augusta quickly. She pulled the top of the crate back into place, and the strongbox key came loose from her shirt. "You won't tell anyone about me?"

"Wait," said Johnny. "The strongbox key! That's what the spy wants!"

Heavy steps sounded nearby. Augusta put her finger to her mouth and backed into the shadows.

The steps got closer.

With each step came a strange flopping sound.

Johnny backed into the shadows next to Augusta.

A voice said, "Johnny, is that you?"

Deane's chubby face appeared above the crates and barrels. "Johnny! Feeling better? I thought I heard you talking. What are you doing back here? I lost both shoe buckles." Deane put his shoes forward. The tongues flopped out.

Johnny asked, "How did you lose both?"

"After I lost the first one, they gave me another chance. Can you believe I rolled a 3 six times in a row?"

Augusta laughed. "They cheated, Deane. They

were probably using weighted dice."

"Weighted?" asked Deane. "How?"

Johnny knew. "If you put weight in one side of the die, the other side come up when you throw it."

Augusta said, "You were playing Hazard? After you saw the same number 4 times, you should have made them choose the main and throw the dice."

Deane nodded. "I'll do that next time."

"Next time?" asked Johnny.

"Of course next time," said Deane. "I still want that ball. What are you doing back here in the hold?"

"Nothing," said Johnny and Augusta at the same time.

Deane raised his eyebrows. "Nothing?"

"Aug – I mean, Gus was showing me where they store the ship's parts," said Johnny.

"And now I need to go. Good luck next time betting against the sailors, Deane," Augusta said.

"Thanks!" answered Deane.

"You're welcome!" answered Augusta sarcastically.

"Johnny, where are the ship's parts? Anything interesting?"

Johnny went to the crate, its top still awry. He pushed it so the top covered Augusta's doll. The other side of the crate came exposed.

Inside were more gleaming brass tubes. There was canvas on top of blackened wood and a large screw. A thick glass like a porthole was on its side. It was all carefully packed in hay and smelled like animal grease.

"That stinks," said Deane. "Let's get to the

quarterdeck."

Johnny felt his stomach rumble again. The rumbling grew louder as Johnny climbed to the quarterdeck. In the clean air topside, Johnny took a deep breath. Full lungs of salt air calmed his stomach.

The British ships still loomed in the distance.

"Are they closer?" asked Deane. "I can't tell."

Vernon appeared with his spyglass. "They are closer. A couple of hundred yards closer. We may get a fight after all!"

Deane looked at Vernon. "Why do you want a fight so bad, Vernon?"

"If the British had taken as much from you as they have from me, you would want revenge, too, Deane," said Vernon.

Johnny asked, "What did the British take from you, Vernon?"

"Our ships," said Vernon. "Those were the first things they took. They took all my father and uncle's ships. Then they burned our house. Burned it to the ground. And they took all of our property, including our slaves."

"Slaves?" repeated Johnny. "You had slaves?"

"Yes, many," said Vernon. "My father's ships took rum and goods to Africa, exchanged them for slaves which went to the Caribbean and the South. Then sugar to New England. We came to own many slaves. Until the British took them and our ships. Which is why I'm going to Europe. There's nothing left for me in America."

"But slaves," repeated Johnny. "Other human beings. How could you own slaves?"

"I just explained it to you, Johnny. What didn't you understand?"

Deane coughed, and Vernon grimaced. "Deane, cover your mouth. You and your sores are disgusting. Johnny, you should stay away from this foul boy."

"I'm not –" started Deane, but he was interrupted by Johnny's father.

"There you are, Johnny," said his father. "Dr. Noel is looking for you. He said your French lessons were to start this morning. He's waiting in his cabin."

Finally, Johnny could ask Dr. Noel about the spy.

"Come on, Deane. Let's go!" Then he stopped. "Where is his cabin?"

"In our hallway, second door on the right," said Johnny's father.

Chapter Eight

Johnny knocked on the second door on the right.

A booming, "*Entrez!*" sounded.

Dr. Noel's cabin was the same size as Johnny's, but it felt cramped. Wall to wall were boxes of books. Leather bindings were open. Ivory pages spilled everywhere. On the bed. On the desk. On the one chair that Dr. Noel wasn't sitting on.

And Dr. Noel himself was large enough to fill up twice as much space as Johnny's father. Dr. Noel pulled the books off the chair. "Please, sit here, Johnny. Deane, sit on the hammock."

Johnny sat. Deane swung in the hammock.

"Please, Mr. Deane," said Dr. Noel.

Deane stopped swinging.

Dr. Noel leaned in close to Johnny. "Now, how you will learn French?"

"I thought you were going to teach us," said Johnny.

"I will speak to you French words, yes. I will give you French books to read, yes. I will listen as you speak French, yes. But I can only teach it. I cannot learn it. That is for you. How you will learn it?"

"I – I don't know," said Johnny. "The same way I learn anything, I guess."

"How is that?"

"I memorize things. I think about them. I don't know. It just happens."

"How do you think about things?"

"I don't know, Dr. Noel," said Johnny. "I just think about them."

"There are two things that separate us from the beasts, boys," said Dr. Noel. "The first is our souls. The second is that we think about thinking. We improve our minds. We become better by thinking about how to think. We learn how to learn."

Deane was confused. "How do we do that?"

"French is a good place to start," said Dr. Noel. "You will look for clues. You will look for structure. You will break apart the structure. You will put it back together again in a better way. That is how you will learn."

Johnny had no idea what Dr. Noel meant. Deane had no idea what Dr. Noel meant. They both nodded anyway.

"Language is also sounds. After you read a page silently, I will read the page to you. You will listen to the sounds. Then you will read the same page out loud. Then you will read it silently again. If you have a question, raise your finger like this." Dr. Noel raised his scarred index finger. His left eyebrow flew up.

Johnny raised his index finger that wasn't scarred.

"Yes?" said Dr. Noel.

"It's not a question, exactly," said Johnny. "But I think I heard the spy talking to a sailor yesterday morning."

"Spy?" repeated Deane. "What spy?"

Dr. Noel's eyes narrowed. "Deane, I have been looking at your sores and can bear the sight no longer. I think a poultice will help. Go to the cook and ask for an onion and a small jar of honey."

Deane stood up reluctantly. "Now?"

"Yes, now," said Dr. Noel.

"All right," said Deane and he was gone.

"Now, Johnny," said Dr. Noel. "What did you hear?"

"Deane knows about the spy," said Johnny.

"What does he know? And what do you know?" asked Dr. Noel.

Johnny took a deep breath. "I heard two men talking the first morning aboard. One told the other to find the secret plans. He said to check the strongbox. But if he finds the plans, he should leave them there."

"Interesting," said Dr. Noel. "He is wrong, but it is interesting."

"Wrong how?" asked Johnny.

"There are no secret plans. No secret plans in the strongbox or anywhere else on this ship."

"No secret plans?" asked Johnny. "How do you know?"

Dr. Noel smiled. "Because I would know if there were. Now, what else did he say?"

"There was more, but . . . I can't remember. Is he the spy you thought was aboard?" asked Johnny.

Dr. Noel went silent for a long moment. Then he

asked, "Did you see him or the man he was talking to?"

"No," said Johnny.

"Anything strange or different about his voice?"

"The spy's voice sounded older than the other man's. And he said 'strongbox' strangely. Like he was swallowing. It was a foreign accent."

Dr. Noel nodded. "What did your father say about this?"

"He said to ignore secret things."

"Your father is a wise man," said Dr. Noel. "You should ignore it."

Johnny was confused. "But you said to everyone last night to watch for the spy. That's what I did!"

"I said for the officers to watch for the spy. Not you."

"But I want to help. What can I do to help?" asked Johnny.

"Nothing," said Dr. Noel. "Ah, there is one thing: Do not tell anyone else."

"But –" started Johnny.

"Not Deane. Not Gus. Not anyone else."

Deane opened the door. He held out a jar of honey and an onion. "Here they are, Dr. Noel!"

"Thank you, Deane." Dr. Noel took out a knife and chopped the onion. In the tight space, the smell of the onion made Johnny's eyes water. Dr. Noel mixed the honey with the onion and put the concoction in a thin rag. "Keep this on the worst of your sores, Deane. But the more important thing is that you get sunlight on your skin as much as possible. Stay on the quarterdeck as much as you can."

"Yes, Doctor," said Deane.

"Now to your French," said Dr. Noel. He handed each of them a book.

Johnny looked at the strange words on the first page. "How do I read this? I don't know any French."

"You know some Latin, yes?" asked Dr. Noel.

"Yes," answered Johnny

"And you know English, yes?" asked Dr. Noel.

"Of course," said Johnny.

"French has many same words as Latin and English. Look for the verbs. Look for names. Look for structure. It is like a boat with parts. But it is not a boat until the parts are put together. Then it can sail. That is how you will learn."

Where to start? Johnny looked for verbs. Could *commence* be one? Like the English word for beginning? Names seemed to be capitalized, like in English. There was Louis XVI, usually next to the word *roi*. And Marie Antoinette. Often next to the word *reine*. *Autriche* was another capitalized word. There was another word like English: *mariage*. Marriage.

"Can you see what it is about?" asked Dr. Noel.

"The marriage of France's King Louis XVI to Marie Antoinette?" asked Johnny. "What is *Autriche*?"

"Austria," answered Dr. Noel.

Johnny looked again at the page. "Marie

Antoinette is from Austria?"

"She is," answered Dr. Noel. "Now listen to me read."

Dr. Noel's scarred forehead wrinkled. His lips pursed. He bent over the book and read.

The sound surprised Johnny. He had expected French to sound the way Dr. Noel spoke English. Rough. Harsh. Guttural. Like words escaping from a cage.

Instead, it sounded like a song. High and low tones. In a rhythm. One word stretched into the next. One sentence flew to the next. When Dr. Noel stopped, it was too soon. Johnny wanted the words to go on.

"Your turn, Johnny," said Dr. Noel, the harsh English tone back.

Johnny read and tried to find the same rhythm he had just heard. It was impossible. Too many stops and starts on unfamiliar words.

"Deane, if you will do the next page, please," said Dr. Noel.

Deane read, listened to Dr. Noel, and read some more.

It gave Johnny a moment to think. A moment to wonder: How did Dr. Noel know there would be a spy aboard the ship?

Then it was Johnny's turn to read again. And listen again. And read again.

At the end of an hour, Johnny was exhausted. So much concentration.

At sunset, Johnny went to the quarterdeck. He saw Vernon standing in a shadow. He was watching the sun dip into the ocean behind the British ships and mouthing words Johnny couldn't hear.

Johnny edged closer and heard Vernon say, "Ships. Home. Slaves."

Vernon said it again. And again. And again.

Johnny moved away.

Deane rushed up to Johnny. "What did you and Dr. Noel talk about while I was getting the poultice? What did Dr. Noel say about the spy?"

JOHN BRADDOCK

Chapter Nine

"I'm not supposed to say," said Johnny.

"You're not supposed to say what?" asked Deane.

"I'm not supposed to say what I'm not supposed to say," said Johnny.

Deane shrugged. "It's all right. My father is on a secret mission that I'm not supposed to talk about either."

"He is?" asked Johnny.

"I heard my uncle talking about it. He's buying weapons in Paris."

"What kind of weapons?" asked Johnny.

"I don't know. That part is really secret. But you don't need to tell me your secret, Johnny. It's all right."

"I would, but – it's not my secret."

"I understand. It's all right," Deane said as he started unbuttoning his shirt.

"What are you doing?" asked Johnny.

Deane pulled his shirttail free. "I'm taking my shirt off. Dr. Noel said to get as much sunlight on my skin as possible. You were there."

Deane pulled his shirt off and turned to face the sun. He had red splotches on his skin and open sores on his arms. "I know," said Deane. "It doesn't look good, but it's not contagious. Vernon hates it. Watch

70

this."

Deane shuffled up to Vernon on the stern, who was still whispering under his breath. Deane coughed, and Vernon turned around.

"Disgusting!" yelled Vernon. "Get your sores away from me, Deane!"

"Oh, I'm sorry, Vernon," said Deane. "I didn't see you there."

Johnny turned so Vernon couldn't see him laugh.

Augusta trudged by carrying rope with two sailors. They went to the forecastle, and Johnny followed.

Now that he knew she was a girl, it was obvious. Why hadn't he seen it before? Why didn't the sailors see it? Johnny stood off to the side and watched her hand rope to the sailors above her. It was obvious.

Watching her work, Johnny remembered she had never answered the question about the strongbox. The strongbox was the one thing he knew the spy wanted to get. And Augusta had the key. She knew what was in it. Which meant she knew what the spy wanted.

Augusta finished on the forecastle and jumped down to the quarterdeck. She walked back to the captain's cabin, and Johnny followed. She went to the stern, and Johnny followed. She went to the back rail, and Johnny followed.

Suddenly, she turned around and pushed Johnny against the gunwale. "What are you doing? Now that you know I'm a girl, do you have some kind of romantic interest?"

"What?" said Johnny. "No, of course not. Of course not! I just wanted to ask you a question about the strongbox."

"All right then," said Augusta. She released Johnny and straightened out his shirt. "Why do you want to know about the strongbox?"

"We know the spy wants what's inside. Secret plans, he said. So what's inside?"

"None of your business," said Augusta. "But I'll tell you because it doesn't matter. The only papers are the ship's log and some paper currency. French and British and Spanish. And a little gold. That's all. No secret plans. Nothing for a spy to want."

"Then why –" Johnny was confused again. "Why did the spy want the strongbox key?"

"It's obvious," said Augusta.

"It is?" said Johnny.

"He wants something he thinks is in the strongbox. What would a spy think is in the strongbox but isn't there?"

The next morning, Johnny woke up tired. His mind had raced all night. He had tossed and turned in his hammock, which banged him into the cabin walls. He thought more about what he knew and what he didn't know.

There were papers in the strongbox that weren't plans. Plans that the spy wanted but weren't there.

And Dr. Noel knew something about them, but they didn't exist.

Johnny's tired mind came to a conclusion: Someone was lying. Either the spy had lied about what he wanted. Or Dr. Noel had lied about there being no plans. Or Augusta was lying about what was in the strongbox.

Someone was lying.

The only way to get the truth would be to find the spy.

Johnny climbed to the quarterdeck to listen to the sailors. Maybe, he would hear the spy talking. Maybe, he could hear the spy say something like "strongbox." Maybe, Johnny would find the spy.

Johnny was standing there for only a moment when Mr. Griffin came up to him. "Idle, Johnny? Do you need a job, Johnny? If so, I've got broken rope that needs re-weaving. Can you help?"

Since it gave Johnny a reason to be near the sailors, Johnny said, "Of course, Mr. Griffin. Happy to help."

"Here you are," said Mr. Griffin. "Pull the strands apart back to the good part, then weave them together tight as you can. So they're strong."

"Aye, aye," said Johnny. He took the strands and pulled them back, then wove them together.

"Good, good," said Mr. Griffin. "How are you getting along with Gus?"

Johnny looked up sharply. "Good. Fine. Good."

"Excellent," said Mr. Griffin. "Gus is a fine lad. A fine lad. As are you, Johnny. Always ready to work.

Always ready to help."

"Thank you," said Johnny.

"You remind me of another lad with me on another voyage. That boy was part of the crew. Hard-working. He got stronger as the voyage went on, just like you. And then he heard a rumor. One of the silly things that sailors talk about. He became obsessed with it. He couldn't think of anything else."

"What was it?" asked Johnny.

"He thought the captain was keeping a secret. A secret that was in the captain's strongbox."

Johnny was silent.

Mr. Griffin continued. "This boy tried to steal the key to the strongbox. Stealing, as you know, is a capital offense on a ship. But the captain let him off easy, since he was just a boy. He kept him in chains the rest of the voyage and dumped him in the first port. We never heard from him again."

Johnny was silent. Was that a warning? Why did Mr. Griffin tell him that story? Johnny didn't know what to say, so he worked harder pulling the rope and weaving it together.

Mr. Griffin tied off the ends. "Now that that's done, Johnny, could you carry the rope to the crow's nest?"

"Of course," said Johnny. He wrapped the rope into a circle and put his head through it.

"Well done, Johnny," said Mr. Griffin. "You're a fine lad."

Johnny grabbed the handholds on the main mast

and lifted himself up. Augusta must have told Mr. Griffin about Johnny's questions about the strongbox. Was Mr. Griffin saying to not ask any more questions about it? That's what it sounded like. But why did Mr. Griffin care?

Johnny continued up the main mast. The rope over his shoulder weighed half as much as he did, and his arms got tired as he climbed higher. Near the top, Johnny could only climb with his legs. His arms were almost useless. He reached the crow's nest with the last of his strength and shoved the rope into the base.

Free of the rope, Johnny stood enjoying the view. Beyond the British ships was a line of clouds that dipped into the horizon. In front of the ship, the sky was cloudless. The sea was smooth and clear as glass.

A sailor below shielded his eyes and cursed. "Mr. Griffin, dead water ahead! Dead water ahead!"

Johnny looked and saw only the clear, glass-like water.

Dead water?

On the quarterdeck, the bell rang.

The captain appeared.

Mr. Griffin and Welch and Barron conferred with him.

Mr. Griffin yelled an order to the masts. "All hands! Pull the sails tight! We need every inch!"

Then, the captain ordered, "Guns at the ready!"

Chapter Ten

Sailors climbed from the hatches and hustled into the masts. Covers flew from the cannons, gunports came open, cannonballs were passed hand to hand. Barrels of gunpowder were opened next to the guns. The pitch-soaked sticks for lighting the cannons were lit. Just as the sailors finished, the *Boston*'s sails fell flat.

The *Boston*'s deck went steady.

Her wake thinned.

Johnny scrambled down the main mast. To avoid the sailors coming up, he stepped out on a spar. There was a loose rope hanging, so Johnny grabbed it and lowered himself. Halfway down, someone pulled the low end of the rope. It made Johnny swing sideways. The rope passed over a cannon crew, and one of them pushed it away. Johnny swung back toward the main mast. A hand grabbed his ankle.

With all her slight weight, Augusta pulled Johnny back. He let himself down hand over hand and dropped to the deck.

"Thank you," said Johnny. "Do you know what's happening?"

"We've hit doldrums," she said.

"What's doldrums?" asked Johnny.

"You don't know?" Augusta shook her head. "I

think you were adopted. It's when the winds go calm and you can't sail. But we have momentum. We're like a stone thrown on a frozen pond. So are the British. We'll see which stone slides furthest."

Vernon arrived with his spyglass. "It's doldrums! Now, we'll have to fight!"

Augusta said, "Don't be so sure, Vernon. If we slide further than the Britisher, there won't be a fight."

"Are you afraid?" mocked Vernon.

"I'm not afraid of a fight," said Augusta, squaring up to Vernon, though her head only came to his shoulder. "Smaller ships beat bigger ones all the time."

Vernon laughed. "Exactly, boy. That's why we should turn and fight now! Come on, Johnny, let's go to the wheel. This will be a lesson on war!"

At the wheel, Lieutenant Welch was alternating between his eyepiece and a notebook. Reading his marks over his shoulder were Captain Tucker, Lt. Barron and Mr. Griffin.

"Come on then, Mr. Welch," said the captain impatiently. "Call it out."

Lieutenant Welch held the scope to his eye for another moment, then said, "The Britisher is at 3000 yards astern, Captain."

The man-o-war's sails drooped as it came close to the line in the sea where the waves went flat. "When the Britisher comes close," said Vernon in Johnny's ear. "The captain will tell us to turn broadside, to face her with our guns. But we can only do that while we move. If we wait too long, we won't be able to turn. The Britisher will go at us with her fore guns, and we'll have no guns pointed at her."

Mr. Griffin called out an order. The sailors pulled all the sails down from the masts. Without wind behind them, the sails could only slow them down. The sailors finished their work, and there was an eerie silence on the quarterdeck. Then Mr. Welch called out, "The Britisher is at 2700 yards astern." He said it loud enough for everyone to hear.

"Marines ready!" called out Captain Tucker.

Johnny shielded his eyes against the setting sun and tried to judge the Britisher's distance by its size. Above, the ramrods of Jamison's Marines slid into their barrels. Their muskets were loaded. The Marines were ready.

"2500 yards astern," called out Mr. Welch in a calm, clear voice.

No waves lapped against the hull. No sails popped in the wind. Not a single word came from the crew.

"2400 yards astern," called Mr. Welch.

"That's close enough, Mr. Welch," said Captain Tucker. "Turn the wheel sixty degrees."

"Aye, Captain," said Mr. Welch. "Turn the wheel sixty degrees."

The helmsman turned the wheel, but the *Boston* continued straight ahead.

"Turn the wheel sixty degrees," repeated Mr. Welch.

"Sir, I did," said the sailor nervously. "There's no response."

"No response? What the devil? Stand aside," said Captain Tucker. He grabbed the wheel and turned it.

The ship didn't turn.

"The wheel's – something's wrong, Mr. Griffin," said Captain Tucker. "See if you can fix it! Hurry!"

"Aye, aye," said Mr. Griffin as he scampered below.

"How close, Mr. Welch?" asked the captain.

"2300 yards, Captain," called out Mr. Welch.

Mr. Griffin reappeared, huffing and out of breath. He said, "Captain! A word, please!"

Captain Tucker ducked next to Mr. Griffin. Johnny leaned in to hear, but caught only an angry, "Confound it!" from the captain and "Can you fix it?"

"Aye," said Mr. Griffin. "But it will take a day or more."

Captain Tucker looked up and scanned the crowd that had gathered around him. His eyes landed on Vernon and narrowed.

Mr. Welch shouted, "2250 yards, Captain!"

"Ready yourselves, men," shouted Captain Tucker. "If it comes to a fight, we'll give these British something to remember us by!"

"Huzzah! Huzzah!" came from the sailors and Marines.

"Captain!" shouted Welch. "The Britisher is 2300 yards astern – she's fallen further back!"

A puff of smoke erupted from the Britisher.

"Captain!" exclaimed Welch, pointing. "They are firing!"

A cannonball arced through the air.

It splashed in the water hundreds of yards short of the *Boston.*

"Well, men," said Captain Tucker with a laugh. "That's one fewer cannonball they can fire at us! One more measurement, Mr. Welch, if you please!"

"2400 yards astern, Captain. They've fallen further back again."

"Thank you, Mr. Welch," said Captain Tucker as another British cannonball splashed into the water.

Captain Tucker shook his head. "Isn't that the British way? They love to fight from far away. That's not bad . . . A good song! Mr. Welch, will you join me?"

Mr. Welch looked like he would rather not, but he did anyway. The Captain waved his arms to the crew and soon the whole ship was singing:

Isn't that the British way?
They love to fight from far away!
Isn't that the British way?
They love to fight from far away!

Soon a song came back at them across the water from the British ship. Johnny heard the word "king," but he couldn't make out the rest of it.

"Gus, invite Dr. Noel and Mr. Adams to my cabin immediately. Mr. Griffin, please join me. And Johnny, you, too, please."

Vernon stood there awkwardly. "Captain. Me, too?"

"I think not immediately, Mr. Vernon, but please be ready. I may need you soon."

Vernon wasn't happy. "I will be in my cabin, then."

When Captain Tucker closed the door behind Johnny and Mr. Griffin, his face was bright red. "Was Mr. Vernon with you, Johnny, the whole time?"

Johnny was confused. "With me?"

"Since the sea change?" asked the captain impatiently.

"Yes. Yes, I think so," said Johnny. "Yes, he was. He was with me. And Gus."

As if she had heard her name, Augusta opened the door. Dr. Noel and Johnny's father followed her in.

"Gus, Mr. Vernon was with you since the sea change?" asked Captain Tucker.

"Yes, he was," answered Augusta.

"Well, what the devil!" exclaimed Captain Tucker.

"What has happened?" asked Johnny's father.

"A wood beam was cut. The beam that goes from the wheel to the rudder," said Mr. Griffin. "We lost our steering just as the British neared."

"Cut?" repeated Dr. Noel, his eyes narrowing.

"It was not Vernon," said Captain Tucker.

Dr. Noel said, "As you know, we had intelligence that a British spy was among the ship's crew. I did not think he would act so soon."

The officers murmured.

Dr. Noel continued, "Johnny has something to say."

Chapter Eleven

Captain Tucker exploded at Dr. Noel. "You didn't think the spy would act so soon?"

Dr. Noel shook his head. "A mistake. I should have known that he would act when the British were close. I should have been watching."

Johnny's father glanced at Johnny and asked, "Is the ship in danger?"

"I think not now, Mr. Adams," said Dr. Noel as he lit his pipe. "I think the spy is not dangerous now."

"Not dangerous?" thundered Captain Tucker. "He sawed through the steering line and nearly caused our capture!"

"That is done, Captain. Now it is time to think about what will happen next." Dr. Noel took a puff of his pipe. "Johnny, what was it you heard him say?"

All eyes in the room turned to Johnny. He looked at Mr. Griffin for help. "I told you what I heard."

"Yes," said Dr. Noel impatiently. "I know. But please, start at the beginning and tell us all what you heard. Go, please, Johnny."

With everyone staring at him, Johnny was nervous. "It was a man with a deep voice talking to another man. The man with the deep voice said he had an arrangement – a special arrangement, he said – with the British. If the other man helped him, the British would treat him well and pay him when they captured the *Boston*."

"I knew the British ships found us too easily!" exclaimed Captain Tucker. "He must have signaled them on the coast."

"Please continue, Johnny," said Dr. Noel.

"He said he had a letter with a seal on it. It would be his proof when the British captured us."

"There you have it!" said Captain Tucker. "We'll search the ship. We find the letter, we find the spy!"

Dr. Noel looked up. "There may be a better way, Captain. A greater opportunity. But is that all, Johnny? Is that all he said?"

Johnny took his mind back to that first night on the ship. The tossing deck. His sick stomach. Sitting against the barrel in the dark.

Johnny remembered something else.

"The sailor talked about a Lord West. I don't remember exactly what he said, but he acted like Lord West was someone powerful. Like Lord West could make the other man rich."

The room went silent.

"What is it?" asked Johnny. "Do you know Lord West?"

Johnny's father spoke. "Johnny, could it have been Lord North you heard him say? Not Lord West?"

"Yes!" exclaimed Johnny. "That's it! It was Lord North."

The men in the room looked down at the floor.

Finally, Dr. Noel spoke. "If this spy is a personal spy of Lord North, it is worse than we thought. He will be crafty and clever and trained in dark things."

Johnny and Gus asked at the same time, "Who is Lord North?"

Captain Tucker ignored them. "We cannot let this stand. Mr. Griffin, order every man to the quarterdeck. We will search the ship for that letter. We will find Lord North's spy."

Mr. Griffin went to the door, but Dr. Noel stopped him. "Captain, please, can we discuss a moment? This is an opportunity."

Captain Tucker took a deep breath. "Tell me, Dr. Noel: How is Lord North's spy on my ship an opportunity?"

"In the larger game, Captain," said Dr. Noel with a puff of his pipe. "We now have an advantage. Lord North's spy does not know we know he is here. I think the Committee would want us to take this opportunity to use Lord North's spy for our purposes."

Captain Tucker looked unconvinced, so Dr. Noel continued, "Lord North's spies follow orders to a fault. The spy aboard will do what he has been told to do. We know one of his orders was to disable our ship if a British ship came close. Without other orders, the spy will not act. That means there is no danger now. There is an opportunity."

"But he may have other orders we do not know about," said Captain Tucker.

"It is true," said Dr. Noel. "However, the opportunity is greater than the risk, as long as we are not near other British ships. As long as the spy does not know we know he is here."

"What is your opinion, Mr. Adams?" asked the captain.

"I trust Dr. Noel's sense in these matters," said Johnny's father.

Captain Tucker nodded.

"No search, Captain?" asked Mr. Griffin at the door.

"No search, yet," repeated Captain Tucker. "And, Mr. Griffin, tell the sailors that the wheel line was snapped, not sawed through, if you please, so the spy does not know we are aware of his presence."

Johnny spoke up. "Respectfully, Captain, you can't say it was snapped. The spy knows the wheel line was sawed through. If he hears you tell everyone that it wasn't, he'll know you're lying. He'll know you're trying to trap him."

There was silence in the cabin.

"Johnny is right," said Dr. Noel through a puff of pipe smoke. "What can we say?"

They all looked at Mr. Griffin.

Mr. Griffin shrugged. "It was sawed through. What can we say?"

Johnny spoke up again. "Can you blame the people who repaired the boat in America? Can you say it was so badly done that there was a clean break?"

Captain Tucker nodded. "Yes, we can, Johnny.

Yes, we can. Mr. Griffin, blame the last repairs in port. Defective equipment. Say the wood was so badly milled that there was a clean break. Almost like someone had sawed it." Captain Tucker winked at Johnny. "You have your orders, Mr. Griffin."

"Yes, sir," said Mr. Griffin.

"But who is Lord North?" asked Johnny. "And what is the Committee?"

Captain Tucker said, "Never mind, Johnny. And Gus, the secret must stay in this room. You'll not mention this to anyone else. Not Vernon. Not Deane. No one."

"Aye, aye," said Augusta.

"Yes, sir," said Johnny.

As soon as the cabin door shut behind them, Johnny asked his father, "Who is Lord North? And what is the Committee?"

Johnny's father sighed. "I'm sorry you heard all that, Johnny. This journey is more dangerous than I thought it would be. Perhaps your mother was right – I should not have brought you."

"Mamma wanted me to come," said Johnny. "She told me."

"At first, she didn't," said Johnny's father. "I persuaded her, and she agreed."

"Who is Lord North?" repeated Johnny. "Why is everyone afraid of him?"

Johnny's father sighed again. "Lord North is the prime minister of England. He has a much-feared spy network. Some say even the king is afraid of it. He uses his spy network for espionage and kidnapping and assassinations to build tyranny."

Johnny said, "I thought we were fighting King George?"

"King George is only the face of the British government," said Johnny's father. "Behind him is a powerful group of criminals. Lords who see colonies as paths to riches. Lords who care nothing for colonists. Lords who consider Americans their slaves. Of the group, some say Lord North is the brains. Some say it is Lord North who really rules, more than King George. His favorite weapon? His spies. His spies are everywhere."

"Even here," said Johnny.

"Even here," agreed Johnny's father. "But enough of that. Dr. Noel says not to worry, so we won't. It's time for your studies. Do you remember the letter I wrote you last summer?"

"Yes, Pappa," said Johnny. "Of course. I memorized it."

"You memorized it?"

"Yes," said Johnny. "Mamma said your letters were too few and far between, so she made me memorize them."

Johnny's father laughed. "That sounds like your mother. Well, then, what did I say?"

"You said:

My dear Son,

As the War in which your Country is engaged will probably hereafter attract your Attention, more than it does at this Time, and as the future Circumstances of your Country, may require other Wars, as well as Councils and Negotiations, similar to those which are now in Agitation, I wish to turn your Thoughts early to such Studies, as will afford you the most solid Instruction and Improvement for the Part which may be allotted you to act on the Stage of Life."

"And what after that?" asked Johnny's father.

"You said to study Thucydides on the Greek wars. And Hobbes. I did it. I read them."

At the time, Johnny had thought it ridiculous. The crops were about to be harvested. A lamb from the spring before hadn't had enough milk. A new batch of chickens weren't laying. Johnny's mother wasn't sure they would have enough food for winter. And his father wanted him to think about wars and councils and negotiations.

Now, Johnny understood what his father had meant. Thucydides helped him understand what was happening between Britain and France and the United States. Hobbes helped him understand the darkness in men's hearts.

"Now," said Johnny's father. "Read them again. Now that you've seen more, they'll speak to you in a different way."

When Johnny went to the quarterdeck the next morning, the *Boston* and the British ship stood the same distance apart. Close enough to hear each other's voices. Far enough away to be out of cannon range. But close enough, Lt. Jamison said, for a surprise attack by skiff, if the British were clever. A watch was kept on the British ship, just in case.

When Johnny went to Dr. Noel's cabin for his French lesson, Johnny found Dr. Noel crouched over his desk with his fingers steepled. At Johnny's knock, Dr. Noel rose and closed the door behind Johnny.

"You are certain you could identify the spy's voice?" asked Dr. Noel.

"I've been trying," said Johnny. "But I need to hear a word like 'strongbox.'"

"Good," nodded Dr. Noel. "That makes eight possibilities instead of seven."

"Possibilities of what?" asked Johnny.

Chapter Twelve

"It is not your concern yet, Johnny," said Dr. Noel.

"Yet?" repeated Johnny. "When will it be my concern?"

Dr. Noel shrugged. "Perhaps never. Perhaps soon. We shall see. For now, you must learn to learn."

"But what is the Committee?"

Dr. Noel sighed. "I can only tell someone of the Committee who can help the Committee."

"I can help!" exclaimed Johnny.

"Perhaps someday, Johnny. Someday but not yet," said Dr. Noel.

Johnny was silent for a moment. "What about Lord North's spy? What will he do next?"

"A good question, Johnny," said Dr. Noel. "Can you figure it out for yourself?"

Johnny thought. The spy wanted secret plans from a strongbox. But Augusta said there were no secret plans in the strongbox. And Dr. Noel said that he was unlikely to act, anyway. What would Lord North's spy do next?

"Do what I told you to do with French," said Dr. Noel. "Take those questions apart. Find the structure underneath. Put the parts of the questions back together as answers."

Johnny shook his head. "I don't understand what you mean. How do I do that?"

Dr. Noel sighed. "I will help you learn how to learn. And I will help you learn French. To do both, you may ask me any question you like, if you can ask it in French."

"But I don't know French!" said Johnny.

Dr. Noel shrugged. "You must learn."

There was a knock on the door. Deane peered in. "Oh, Johnny, you're already here. Sorry, I'm late, Dr. Noel."

"Sit down, Deane. Johnny, open your book and read," said Dr. Noel.

After four days in the doldrums, Johnny had almost figured out the structure of French enough to ask a question. The words for who, what, where, when and why were simple enough: *Qui, Que, Ou, Quand*, and *Pourquoi*. But they blended together with verbs and sometimes you had to put another word before the object.

And there was something that made it hard to think and figure things out: the stink.

The animals, too many people packed close together and stagnant air combined into something Johnny had never smelled before. The disgusting air hung over the *Boston* like an old blanket on a wet dog.

Johnny took his lunch to the quarterdeck.

Lieutenant Jamison was drilling the Marines. He took them through mock firing, mock reloading, and mock firing again. Then, he told three of them to climb the masts and tossed an old barrel in the water.

When the barrel had floated fifty yards away, Lieutenant Jamison gave the order to fire.

Johnny covered his ears and watched puffs of smoke come from the Marines in the masts.

Two rounds plunked the barrel. The third splashed short.

"A man is smaller than a barrel, Mr. Thomas!" yelled Lieutenant Jamison. "If you can't hit the barrel, you can't hit the man!"

An apology came from the main mast. There was furious pouring of gunpowder and reloading.

Three shots came from the masts again.

This time, three shots hit the barrel.

Vernon was watching. "Lieutenant," Vernon said. "I would be ready for a fight, as well. Please give me one of your men's rifles."

"Do you have any experience with these weapons, Mr. Vernon?" asked Jamison.

"Of course," said Vernon. "I have many rifles at home. My father made certain I knew how to fire them."

Jamison nodded at the nearest Marine. "Give your weapon to Mr. Vernon."

"Thank you," said Vernon. He took the rifle to the side and placed the barrel on the gunwale. He sighted along the barrel. Johnny covered his ears.

Vernon pulled the trigger.

Nothing happened.

Vernon turned the rifle sideways and stood up. Redfaced, Vernon said, "What is this?"

Jamison barely suppressed a smile. "It's not loaded, Mr. Vernon. Would you like to load it?"

Vernon's face turned crimson. "Please load it for me, Lieutenant."

Jamison nodded to the nearest Marine. "Give Mr. Vernon your ball and powder."

Vernon repeated, "Please load it for me, Lieutenant."

Jamison shook his head. "Everyone loads their own weapons, Mr. Vernon. Or maybe you don't know how? Did your servants in Rhode Island load your rifles for you?"

Johnny saw Vernon's face change again. Deep red with anger. "Lieutenant Jamison, you are a Marine in the United States Navy, of which my father is Commissioner. Your insouciance is noted."

"My what?" laughed Jamison. "Your father should have taught you that you can't fire a weapon without knowing how to load it first."

Vernon lifted the rifle in front of him and dropped it.

The rifle hit the deck. It bounced once.

It turned on its side and the hammer released.

The rifle boomed.

A bullet struck the gunwale.

For a moment, there was silence.

Vernon said, "It was loaded?"

Lieutenant Jamison said, "It was loaded?" He turned toward the Marine whose weapon it was.

The Marine said, "I'm sorry, sir. I thought you knew."

"You gave a loaded weapon to a boy?" asked Jamison.

"A boy?" repeated Vernon. "A boy?"

"A boy," repeated Jamison. "Who should leave the fighting to the men who know how to operate weapons. Leave us."

Vernon yelled, "Insouciance!" and went below.

From behind Johnny came a giggle.

It was Augusta. She shook her head. "Insouciance? Insouciance? He thinks big words mean a big brain. I'd put half the crew and all the officers above Vernon when it comes to the size of his brain."

Johnny pulled Augusta aside. "Will you help me with something? I want to see if I can find the spy."

"How?" asked Augusta.

"If you and I get next to a group and mention the strongbox, we can see if any of them are interested."

Augusta smiled and nodded. "Yes, I'll help."

"All right," said Johnny. "Let's go."

A clump of sailors was by the gunwale under the forecastle. Johnny stopped next to them and said to Augusta, "Gus, what did you say was in the strongbox?"

Gus acted surprised. "What do you mean,

Johnny?"

Out of the corner of his eye, Johnny saw one of the sailors at the gunwale turn and listen.

"You said that thing was under lock and key," said Johnny. He turned to get a better look at the sailor who was listening.

"I said –" at that, Augusta leaned forward and whispered in Johnny's ear, "Is it working?"

Johnny stepped back and saw another two sailors were listening. "Oh, that's interesting, Gus," said Johnny quickly. "But if that's what it is, why is it there?"

Six more sailors shuffled closer. Gus said, "It's because –" she stepped forward and whispered again to Johnny, "How many are there?"

Now, a dozen sailors crowded around Johnny and Gus. Four more were listening from the forecastle above.

Augusta suppressed a laugh. "Come on, Johnny, the captain needs me."

At the captain's door, Augusta let out a laugh. "I thought that might happen. Every sailor wants to know what's in the captain's strongbox."

Johnny felt silly. "Why didn't you say so?"

"I thought it would be funny. Sorry."

After dinner, there was a small change in the air. The wet blanket of stink was still there, but more salt was mixed in. It smelled more like seawater than men.

Dr. Noel had skipped the captain's dinner. Deane wanted to gamble with the sailors, but he couldn't stand the stench below. The time in the doldrums had given Deane time to sun himself. His sores were getting smaller. Even Vernon had noticed. When Deane went to the kitchen to steal his second dinner, Johnny went to Dr. Noel's cabin.

He was ready to ask his first question in French.

Chapter Thirteen

Johnny knocked on Dr. Noel's door and said, "I'm ready to ask a question in French."

Dr. Noel didn't look up from his desk. "What is it?"

"*Que fait le comité?*" asked Johnny.

Dr. Noel turned and looked at Johnny. "What does the Committee do? I told you I can't tell you about the Committee."

"I thought – I thought you could tell me what the Committee does, not what it is," said Johnny.

"No," said Dr. Noel. "Not even that."

Dr. Noel looked long at Johnny. "Because I cannot answer that question, you may have another, if you can ask it in French."

Johnny was frustrated. He asked, "What is the French word for scar?"

"Is that your question? You can answer it with a dictionary," said Dr. Noel.

"No – that's not my question," said Johnny. He took the French dictionary from Dr. Noel's desk and thumbed through it until he found the word he was looking for: *cicatrice*. But Johnny had another problem.

"I don't know how to say 'got' – the past tense of 'get,'" said Johnny.

"It depends on what you are asking," said Dr. Noel.

"I want to ask, 'Where did you get your scars?'" said Johnny.

"You break the verb into two parts," said Dr. Noel. "*'Où avez-vous eu vos cicatrices?'*"

Johnny repeated the strange sounds. *"Où avez-vous eu vos cicatrices?"*

"It is a long story," answered Dr. Noel.

"Did the British give them to you?" asked Johnny.

"One question at a time, Johnny. One question at a time."

Johnny suddenly felt sorry for asking. "You don't need to tell me, if you don't want to."

"You should always ask questions. Even if other people don't want to answer them. But this one I do not mind answering. It started because I was a headstrong boy. I was much like Mr. Vernon, I'm sorry to say. I joined the French army and fought the British in India. A place called Pondicherry. We were besieged in a fortress and nearly starved to death. When we surrendered, the British were very cruel. I was beaten many times across my face. Across my arms, my hands and my back. It was all very bad, I am told, but I do not remember. I was left for dead."

"How did you survive?" asked Johnny.

"Ask the question in French," said Dr. Noel.

Johnny grabbed the French dictionary and found the right words. *"Comment avez-vous survécu?* Did I say that right?"

Dr. Noel nodded. "I survived because a Scottish missionary found me. He nursed me back to health, but he wanted something in return. Scots drive a hard bargain, you know. His price for nursing me back to health: I had to read a section of the Bible every day. Every day the same section: The third chapter of Paul's letter to Titus. Do you know it?"

"I don't have it memorized," said Johnny.

"I do – in English and in French. Here is the English version: 'For we ourselves also were sometimes foolish, disobedient, deceived, serving diverse lusts and pleasures, living in malice and envy, hateful, and hating one another. But after that the kindness and love of God our Savior toward man appeared. Not by works of righteousness which we have done, but according to his mercy he saved us.' Every day I read those words. The Bible is a strange book. A frightening book. When you read it, it comes alive. I think the Scot knew that. For three months, I read that every day until my wounds were healed. These scars replaced them. That is how I came by these scars."

A shudder went through the ship. The cabin walls creaked under pressure. The *Boston* rocked back and forth. For the first time in days, the ship was moving.

There were shouts on the quarterdeck. Mr. Griffin gave the order to raise the main sails.

"Ah," said Dr. Noel. "The wind is back. We move again. Now, *on recommence ton lecons en Francais.*"

"But the British ship. It's –" Johnny was cut off by

a great boom. It was followed by a violent crash as something struck the ship. Johnny fell off his chair and into the cabin wall. Through the ceiling, panicked shouts came. Someone ordered the cannons taken below.

Taken below? Thought Johnny. The British are firing on us. Why take the cannons below?

"It is a storm," said Dr. Noel, as if he could read Johnny's thoughts. "Not the British ship."

On the deck, the bell clanged, summoning all hands. The shouts of Captain Tucker, Lieutenant Barron, Lieutenant Welch, and Mr. Griffin came through the ceiling.

"Come on, Dr. Noel!" said Johnny. "Let's go help!"

Johnny climbed to the hatch. He could barely slide it open, as if some force were pushing and bending the wood. When it went open, Johnny was pelted with rain.

Johnny was nearly knocked over by the wind. A bolt of lightning went through the air, joined by an enormous boom. Johnny ducked down. Sailors pulled the cannons back from the gunports and ferried the cannonballs below. Using ropes and pulleys, the sailors swung the cannons into open hatches.

A cannon came loose by the main mast. It flew back and forth, and sailors flattened against the deck. Before the cannon could swing back a third time, a sailor climbed on the spar and slowed the rope's swing with his grip. On its next pass, the other sailors grabbed the cannon and stopped it. Slipping on the wet deck, they lowered it to the hold.

Dr. Noel was right – it was a storm. But where were the British?

Johnny stood and couldn't see far through thick sheets of rain. Vernon was on the stern, hooded in his cloak. His fist was raised, and he looked like he was shouting, but Johnny couldn't hear his words above the wind.

Retreating to the companion hatch, Johnny pulled it partly closed over him and stood on the stairs to watch the sailors work. The sails that had been raised only a short time before came down, and the sailors scurried down the rain-slick masts.

Something like a punch hit Johnny in the face. He fell backward and landed at the bottom of the stairs. His ears were ringing. He came up on his elbows, disoriented and found himself looking into Dr. Noel's face.

"What happened?" asked Dr. Noel.

"I don't know," answered Johnny groggily. "Something hit me."

Dr. Noel raced up the stairs into the rain. Johnny shook his head clear and followed him to the quarterdeck.

There were bodies everywhere.

Chapter Fourteen

Most of the bodies started to move. The sailors got to their hands and knees, stunned by what had hit them. By the main mast, one sailor didn't move . Mr. Griffin put his bare feet carefully on the heaving, rain-slick deck and picked him up. He shouted orders.

Vernon arrived and yelled excitedly, "Did you see the British ship? Where are they?"

The rain was too thick. The darkness had closed in. No one could see.

The main mast was charred and smoking. The top of it was gone. "Was it lightning?" asked Johnny.

"A British cannonball could have done that!" yelled Vernon.

The sea had risen with the storm. Waves crashed over the gunwale. Foamy water fell on the dipping forecastle and spread over the deck. Mr. Griffin caught Dr. Noel's shoulder and handed him the unconscious sailor. Dr. Noel turned and motioned for Johnny.

Gingerly, Johnny stepped on the wet deck. He kept his legs apart, like a circus performer on a wire. Dr. Noel waved at Johnny more urgently and Johnny slid in the water toward Dr. Noel. "Get my bag!" yelled Dr. Noel.

Johnny yelled, "Where is it?" but Dr. Noel was gone, carrying the injured sailor toward the main hold.

Johnny went to Dr. Noel's cabin and found the black leather medical bag. He ran into the hallway and collided with Deane.

"Johnny!" exclaimed Deane. "What's happening?"

"Lightning struck the ship! Dr. Noel needs his medical bag!" said Johnny breathlessly. He ran past Deane with the bag on his shoulder. At the main hatch, the last of the injured were being carried below. Sailors on the starboard side were lowering the final cannons. Johnny balanced and ran down the steps into the main hold.

Captain Tucker and Lt. Barron were inside the gunpowder room examining a large crack in the base of the main mast. "Mr. Barron, keep the foresail up and instruct Lt. Welch to keep this heading. We cannot repair in the storm. We'll ride it out as she is."

A scream came from the kitchen. Over a bleeding sailor was Dr. Noel, moving faster than Johnny thought possible. The sailor had a grotesque hole in his head. Another hole in his leg was bleeding like a plug had been pulled from a bottle. His eyes were wild. He was screaming. He smelled like burnt hair.

Dr. Noel stuffed the sailor's mouth with cloth and said to Johnny, "Saw! I need the saw!"

Johnny opened the black bag. There were straight edge knives. There were pliers. There were clamps. At the bottom was a knife with jagged teeth. It didn't look like a normal saw but was the closest thing. Johnny handed it to Dr. Noel.

Mr. Griffin arrived. "He was touching the cannon when the lightning struck, Dr. Noel. The rest of us felt only the shock." The sailor spit out the cloth and screamed again. Mr. Griffin stuffed the cloth back in. The sailor's muscles tightened. His back arched and his body went limp.

"The brain," said Dr. Noel, dropping all the saws but one. "The pressure is too much." Dr. Noel put his saw to the sailor's head. Johnny couldn't watch.

Blood streamed out of the hole in the sailor's leg. "Mr. Griffin!" said Dr. Noel. "While I cut, you must go inside the hole in the leg. Find the artery and hold it closed!"

"Aye, aye!" said Mr. Griffin. He tried to put his hand in the bloody hole, but only two fingers fit inside.

"Your hand is too big," said Dr. Noel. "Johnny, you do it! Inside the leg is a tube spraying blood. Find the biggest one and squeeze it!"

The last time Johnny had seen a bloody mess like this was his own finger. Johnny took a deep breath and pushed that finger and the rest of his hand into the gooey red flesh. Johnny pushed his fingers deeper. He found a slippery tube. He squeezed, but it slipped. Johnny gripped it again and squeezed it tight.

The blood slowed to a trickle.

Dr. Noel sawed through the skull bone, and the sailor's eyes fluttered open. He spit out the cloth and yelled, "It wasn't my – Mermaids! Three off the starboard bow! The Captain knows! You'll hang!"

The sailor's eyes widened. His chest dropped and his mouth opened. He sank down against the table. A last breath passed his lips.

Dr. Noel climbed on the table. He slapped the sailor's cheeks. No response. He pushed on the sailor's chest one, two, three times. It didn't move. Blood trickled from the head wound and the hole in the leg.

Dr. Noel wiped his brow. "It is done. Johnny, you can let go. He is dead."

Johnny pulled his hand free. Blood streamed out the open wound.

"A pity," said Mr. Griffin. "He was a first-class mate."

Johnny stared at the dead sailor. He was like a solid ghost with dark pale skin. His hands were limp. He moved lifelessly when the ship tossed from side to side.

"On to the floor, on this canvas, before he falls, lift him," said Mr. Griffin. Dr. Noel took both arms. Johnny and Mr. Griffin each grabbed a leg. As Johnny lifted, an edge of paper showed from the man's pants pocket.

Dr. Noel saw it, too. "Pull it out, Johnny."

Johnny gingerly grabbed the edge of paper and pulled it free. It had bloody fingerprints on it.

"It has a wax seal," said Johnny. "And some writing."

"Read it," said Dr. Noel.

Johnny read:

> To all Loyal Subjects of His Majesty George the
> Third, by the Grace of God, King of Great Britain,
> France, and Ireland, Defender of the Faith, Greetings.
> The Bearer of this Letter is an Agent . . .

Dr. Noel stopped him. "I will take it, Johnny." He took the sheet, read it, folded it, and put it away.

"What does the rest say?" asked Johnny.

Dr. Noel looked at Johnny with a smile. "Not of your concern. Thank you for your help, Johnny. I will see to preparation of the body. You may leave."

"But Dr. Noel - " started Johnny.

"Please, Johnny," said Dr. Noel quickly. "We will talk later."

On the way out of the kitchen, Johnny ran into a clump of sailors looking at the cracked main mast.

"There's a curse on the ship, I tell you," said a gray-whiskered man with a black ponytail. "I felt it when I came on board."

"Aye," said another with a scar from eye to jaw. "I did, too."

"It's terrible bad luck the Britishers found us right off the coast, then chased us. And then the doldrums and now this storm. We've been so unlucky, there must be a woman aboard."

"Aye," said Augusta to the sailors. "There's always a woman to blame when luck's this bad."

"Wise words from one so young, Gus," said the gray-whiskered man.

"Aye," "Aye," "Aye," said the rest of the sailors.

Johnny stifled a laugh and went to the main hatch. Rain fell sideways as Johnny stumbled to the companion hatch. Midway there, Vernon passed by with rope in his arms.

"Where are you going?" yelled Johnny.

"To keep watch for the British!" yelled Vernon. Vernon tied himself to the mizzenmast and yelled something into the storm.

Johnny closed the hatch and saw candlelight under his door. Inside, Johnny's father was writing. One hand held a quill. The other held the inkpot and paper on the tilting desk. Johnny's father didn't look up when Johnny came in. "Everything all right, Johnny?"

"Dr. Noel found the spy. And – and the spy died," said Johnny.

"You see," said Johnny's father. "Secret things come to bad ends."

"Yes, Pappa," said Johnny as he shrugged off his wet coat. He crawled into his hammock.

"Did the captain say anything about bathing and cleaning the crew? I saw sickness kill more of our Continental Army than battle. I don't want that to happen to our Navy."

"No, Pappa. He didn't," said Johnny as he pulled the wool blanket to his chin.

"I'll remind him then," said Johnny's father.

His father was always thinking about the most

uninteresting things. Bathing? Cleanliness? What about the dead spy? What would happen now to Dr. Noel's plan? Whatever it had been, he had wanted to use the spy for the Committee's purposes. Whatever the Committee was. Whatever those purposes were. Now, it wouldn't happen because the spy was dead. But why had Dr. Noel smiled when he saw the letter? Was something else happening?

Always more questions with Dr. Noel.

Never an answer.

Johnny sighed, closed his eyes, and drifted off to sleep.

For six days, the ship was tossed by the storm. Without the main mast, there was no hope of sailing out of it. Helmsmen trying to keep the ship's bow toward the biggest waves were changed every hour due to exhaustion.

All the sailors became sick, even Mr. Griffin. He did his duties doubled over, with a pot close in case. The cook changed the ship's meals to a mash of corn and beans and milk to help the sailors eat. The new diet made everyone even more miserable.

No one except a few sailors and Mr. Griffin were allowed above decks in the storm, but Vernon ignored the order. He stayed on the stern, tied to the mizzenmast, keeping watch for the Britishers. When he came below for meals, he ignored everyone, ate quickly and returned to continue his watch.

On the seventh day, the storm subsided.

When the sailors rose to the quarterdeck, they

looked like ghosts. Their clothes were loose from the weight they'd lost. Their hair was wild. Their feet shuffled and dragged.

The weakened crew repaired the main mast with spare timber. The spars were put in place. The ropes were attached. The sails billowed and caught the wind.

The *Boston* was back underway.

Vernon was disappointed. "No sign of the Britishers, Johnny," said Vernon. "No sign of them anywhere!"

With the *Boston* underway, Mr. Griffin ordered the bell rung and all hands to the quarterdeck for a word from the captain.

Johnny was against the gunwale when Dr. Noel brushed by. "Watch closely, Johnny, and tell me what you see."

Johnny started to ask what he should watch for, but Augusta grabbed his arm. "You survived the storm, Johnny? Not too sick?"

"Where were you?" asked Johnny. "I didn't see you. Worried the sailors might blame you for the bad luck?"

"Shhhh!" said Augusta. "You promised to be quiet."

"Sorry," chuckled Johnny.

"Stop it!" said Augusta.

Captain Tucker leaped to the forecastle and turned to the crew. "Men, we've had bad luck this journey. We've been driven off course. Where? We don't yet know. If we're too far north, we'll be in British waters. If we're too far south, there's danger from pirates. Do your duty and keep your eyes on the horizon."

A murmur went through the sailors.

Captain Tucker continued. "There's something worse, men: A British spy was aboard this ship."

Chapter Fifteen

The captain continued, "The spy was killed in the lightning strike. Divine justice, perhaps."

Another murmur ran through the crew.

Dr. Noel watched from his perch next to Captain Tucker.

Deane sidled up next to Johnny. "The spy was killed by lightning! Can you imagine?"

Johnny ignored Deane and tried to listen to the captain's next words. "Now, then, this is no pleasure cruise, men. We carry important cargo on an important mission for our United States. We're at war, men. To be sure you understand exactly what that means, Mr. Barron will now read the Articles of War, as approved by the Congress."

"My father wrote this," said Deane proudly.

Mr. Barron's voice sounded over the sailors. "Whereas his Majesty's most faithful subjects in these Colonies are reduced to a dangerous and critical situation, by the attempts of the British Ministry, to carry into execution, by force of arms, several unconstitutional and oppressive acts of the British parliament for laying taxes in America, to enforce the collection of these taxes, and for altering and changing the constitution and internal police of some of these Colonies, in violation of the natural and civil rights of the Colonies . . ."

"Your father wrote the Articles of War?" asked Johnny.

"Right after Bunker Hill," said Deane.

Mr. Barron continued, " . . . which hath rendered it necessary, and an indispensable duty, for the express purpose of securing and defending these Colonies, and preserving them in safety against all attempts to carry the said acts into execution; that an armed force be raised sufficient to defeat such hostile designs, and preserve and defend the lives, liberties and immunities of the Colonists . . ."

"Then he went to France. That was two years ago. Before Dr. Franklin went," said Deane.

"Did your mother go with him?" asked Johnny.

"No. She died when I was four," answered Deane.

"I'm sorry," said Johnny. "I didn't know."

Deane shrugged. "It's been a long time."

". . . It is earnestly recommended to all officers and soldiers, diligently to attend Divine Service; and all officers and soldiers who shall behave indecently or irreverently at any place of Divine Worship, shall, if commissioned officers, be brought before a court-martial . . ."

"Is he going to read the whole thing?" asked Deane. "It's pretty long."

Mr. Barron read the whole thing. The rest of it was for the soldiers and officers, telling them to not fight amongst themselves, to respect each other, and to not get involved in mutinies or desert their posts.

After Mr. Barron was finished, Captain Tucker ordered everyone on the quarterdeck to squeeze toward the forecastle. He said he wanted to see if the weight changed the way the *Boston* sailed under the new main mast. After two turns, he ordered everyone go to the stern and put their weight in the back. Johnny couldn't tell a difference, but Captain Tucker was happy with the experiment.

"All hands to battle quarters!" came the next call from Captain Tucker. Sailors raced to the cannons, brought the gunpowder and cannonballs from the hold. Marines climbed into the sails with loaded rifles.

Mr. Griffin threw three wooden crates in the water. Mr. Welch ordered another turn of the ship and told the rest of the sailors to shift their weight to the stern.

For the next hour, the *Boston* practiced maneuvering by cutting across the wooden crates. Then, Lt. Barron ordered an attack on the crates. The first shots missed by a hundred yards, but circling around again, the next shots were closer. On the third turn, the crates were blown to splinters. The *Boston* closed in on them, and the Marines in the masts peppered the splintered crates with bullets.

Vernon was happy. "Finally, the Captain is serious. He prepares the ship for war!" The battle against the crates won, the captain ordered the guns cleaned, then all hands to the quarterdeck for another announcement.

Augusta whispered to Johnny. "I'm going to leave soon."

"Why?" asked Johnny.

"You'll see."

Captain Tucker cleared his throat on the forecastle. "Men, you've heard the Articles of War and you've exercised the guns. Now, it's time to exercise your bodies. Bring out the instruments, Mr. Griffin."

"Aye, aye, sir," said Mr. Griffin with a smile. The instruments he brought out, Johnny was surprised to see, were musical instruments. He handed three fiddles, two bells and a drum to sailors who knew how to hold them. The fiddles went to their shoulders and the bells and drum to their hands. Seconds later, a rhythmic song filled the air.

"Now, men," said Captain Tucker. "Your orders are to dance!"

The sailors split into groups of eight, hands together in the middle. As the fiddles started, the sailors stomped in a circle, first one way, then the other.

Deane was pulled into a circle of dancing sailors. He twirled to the music, his bulky frame twisting wildly among the sailors. He called out, "Come on, Johnny! Come on, Gus! Join in!"

"Thanks, Deane, but I'll watch," said Johnny.

Augusta whispered to Johnny, "He doesn't know what's about to happen."

Deane continued his turn, knocking over two nearby sailors. The collision seemed to give other

115

sailors an idea. Soon dancers were tripping and falling all over the quarterdeck. A punch was thrown before Mr. Griffin stepped in. He held back two sailors and got everyone dancing again.

Augusta edged closer to the stern. "It's supposed to be the Miller dance, if you can call it a dance at all. I've never seen it done so badly."

"It shouldn't be done at all!" exclaimed Vernon. "How can we expect to win a war when our sailors act so disgustingly! When my father hears about this, there will be . . . there will be – Captain Tucker will pay!"

"He'll pay what?" asked Augusta. "Your father has given the captain charge of this ship, and he decides what the sailors need."

"Who are you – a cabin boy? To talk to me like that?" sneered Vernon. "Do you know who I am?"

"I know you don't know as much as you think you do," answered Augusta calmly. "Watch what happens when the dance is done."

Mr. Griffin stopped the musicians. "Hold on, there, men! That's enough! Captain, your next orders?"

At the stern, the captain said, "Mr. Cook?"

The cook appeared with six men rolling barrels. They spread around the quarterdeck, turned the barrels upright and packed the sailors together between them.

The cook said, "We're ready, Captain."

"Now!" said Captain Tucker.

The cook and his assistant popped off the barrel tops and dipped their hands in. They pulled out a white powder and flung it high in the air. Scoop after scoop fell on the sailors. The sailors danced in the white cloud, and everyone was covered in it.

"Is that flour?" coughed Johnny.

"Aye, it is," said Augusta in her best imitation of a sailor. "What do you think now, Mr. Vernon?"

"It's – it's an abomination!" stuttered Vernon, even more angry than before. "Wasting food this way!"

"It has a purpose," said Augusta. "We've been nearly a month at sea and some of the sailors haven't changed their clothes once. We've gone through a hurricane and most of the sailors have been sick and everything they have is disgusting. The captain could force the sailors to take baths and change their clothes, or he could do this: get them so crusted and dirty with flour, they'll want to do it themselves."

Deane loved it. He danced, his hair wet and sticking to his scalp in a floured mess. He shed his shirt and shoes and everything else but his breeches.

"Why aren't you with them, then Gus?" asked Vernon. "Why don't you go down and get covered in flour like the rest of them?"

"The captain can't stand a smell in his cabin," said Augusta quickly. "I wash daily."

Vernon wasn't listening. "It's disgusting. If the sailors won't follow orders to stay clean, a good court martial or a hanging would do the trick. Discipline must be maintained, no matter what! We will never

win a war with ships run by men like Tucker and
sailors like this!"

Johnny could see Augusta was about to say
something she might regret, so he interrupted by
pointing to the horizon. "Is that a British sail?"

Vernon turned. "Where? Where? I don't see it!"

"I thought I saw one," shrugged Johnny. "Check
with your spyglass."

With that, Vernon was gone to the forecastle.

Augusta rolled her eyes and said, "He's so – so . . .
Ugh! He thinks he knows so much more than
anybody else! He probably thinks he should be
Captain!"

Mr. Griffin shouted another order. "Every man,
down to his breeches!"

Deane started to take off his pants.

"This is when I leave," whispered Augusta.

The cook rolled out new barrels full of water.
Using buckets, he and his assistants showered the
crew. Deane laughed and danced some more,
knocking two thin sailors over. He apologized and
helped them up.

Johnny noticed that Dr. Noel had slipped away.

Johnny went to Dr. Noel's room and knocked on
his door.

"Ah, Johnny," said Dr. Noel. "What did you see?"

Chapter Sixteen

"What was I looking for?" asked Johnny.

"Something strange. Anything strange. Did you see anything strange?"

Johnny shook his head. "No. Nothing strange, Dr. Noel."

"This spy is talented. It was to be expected of one of Lord North's spies, but I hoped anyway," said Dr. Noel.

Johnny was lost. "What do you mean? The spy's alive?"

"Of course," said Dr. Noel. "We have moved a piece on the board. Hopefully, the spy thinks he's safe."

"But the letter in the dead man's pocket!"

"He thought we were getting too close," Dr. Noel said. "He put the one thing that would allow us to find him in the pocket of the dead man. To make us think the dead man was the spy. Perhaps he has some other way of telling the British which side he is on. I do not know. But that way of finding him is now lost. Clever."

"What —" Johnny didn't know where to start. "What do we do now?"

"As I said, we have moved a piece on the board. The spy thinks he is safe."

"What will happen next?" asked Johnny.

"What do you think will happen next?" asked Dr. Noel.

"I – I don't know. What are the secret plans he's after?"

"Ah," said Dr. Noel. "Now you ask a good question. But there are many questions before that."

"What questions?" asked Johnny.

Dr. Noel was silent for a moment. "What is better? That you solve a riddle or that you have a mind that solves many riddles?"

Reluctantly, Johnny said, "A mind that solves many riddles."

"I agree," nodded Dr. Noel. "Solving a riddle starts with asking the right questions. You should be asking what Lord North's spy would want. To get there, you should ask what the British fear most. To answer that, ask, 'What is the greatest strength of the British?' Then, reason backward to what Lord North's spy would want."

Johnny was confused. "What was the first question to answer? The one about the greatest strength of the British?"

"Yes," said Dr. Noel. "Answer that question first. The other answers will follow."

"Does this have to do with the Committee?" asked Johnny.

Dr. Noel smiled. "Answer the first question first, and we will see if you can be of use to the Committee."

The next day Johnny was no closer to an answer, so he decided to ask his father.

Johnny acted like he was reading Plutarch until his father put down his quill and looked at the cabin wall.

"Pappa," said Johnny. "What do you think is the greatest strength of the British?"

Johnny's father turned around. "An interesting

question, Johnny. An important question. Why do you ask?"

"I was just wondering," said Johnny weakly.

"I believe the greatest strength of the British is their power over men's minds," said Johnny's father. "Many Americans, like our neighbor Mr. Hanford, think men must be ruled by kings. They think there must be a hierarchy. Like we are a pack of dogs that must be kept in order. They think freedom is dangerous."

"How can freedom be dangerous?" asked Johnny. "It's – it's just freedom."

"It's strange, but many are afraid of freedom and the responsibility that comes with it. They would rather be under the king because they know what it's like. It's comfortable. It feels safe. The greatest strength of the British is the mindset of people accepting the king's rule."

"How do we stop it?" asked Johnny.

"We persuade people," said Johnny's father. "We write articles. We publish pamphlets. We speak to crowds. We break the power of the mindset through words. That is why I work so hard on these letters. That is why I write and write and write."

Johnny was silent.

"It is a battle you will wage one day, Johnny. That is why you must read your Plutarch and your Cicero and your ancient books," continued Johnny's father. "To see the arguments made in the past against men's mindset of slavery. To see how to win this battle against slavery that has been fought many times."

Johnny was confused. If the greatest strength of the British was their power over men's minds, then what did they fear? And how did what they fear connect to the spy? And how did it connect to the secret plans?

Johnny couldn't see it.

The next day, Johnny told Dr. Noel what his father had said.

Dr. Noel smiled. "Your father is right, Johnny. You have an answer to the question that I told you to answer."

"How does power over men's minds tell us what the spy will do next?"

"It does not," said Dr. Noel. "Because there is a problem."

"What problem?" asked Johnny.

"Your answer – your father's answer – is not the answer the British would give to the same question," said Dr. Noel.

"There are two answers? I don't understand," said Johnny.

"When you are trying to see what someone will do next, you must see the world the way they see it. You must think the way they would think. You must see with their eyes. You must answer the question of greatest strength the way they would answer. Now, do that."

"Do what?" asked Johnny.

"Answer the question of greatest strength not the way an American would answer it. Not the way your father would answer it. Answer the question of greatest strength the way Lord North and his spy would answer it."

"I – I don't know how," said Johnny.

"Learn how," said Dr. Noel. "No more questions until you can answer that one."

Nine days later, Johnny was no closer to an

answer.

Taking his breakfast on the deck, Johnny saw several sailors struggling with a sail at the top of the main mast. Johnny asked Mr. Griffin if he could help.

With a twinkle in his eye, Mr. Griffin said, "We could use someone not too heavy up at the top of the mast, who could pull from that direction."

"I'll be there in five seconds." Johnny kicked off his shoes and scampered to the top. Johnny took the edge of the sail, then held it as the other sailors moved above him. As they tied the knots, Johnny tried to follow the system being tied. When it was secured, the sail filled with wind.

From his perch, Johnny could see for miles. He felt the fresh breeze and the salt air. Behind him came the pop of the sail's canvas bucking in the wind. Then, he saw a break in the flat line of the horizon.

Squinting as he moved out on the yard, Johnny saw what looked like a piece of paper bobbing on the sea.

A ship!

"Mr. Griffin – a ship – a ship on the horizon!" yelled Johnny.

Chapter Seventeen

"What flag, Johnny?" asked Mr. Griffin.

The topsail filled with wind and blocked Johnny's view. "I can't . . . I can't see."

Lieutenant Welch climbed to the forecastle with his spyglass. "British flag! An armed frigate."

A buzz went through the ship. Captain Tucker came at a run and climbed to the forecastle. Augusta and Vernon arrived as Johnny dropped to the deck.

"How many guns, Mr. Welch?" asked the captain.

"I count twelve, Captain," answered Welch.

"Twelve guns against our twenty-four," mused the captain. "Their bow is aimed toward our shores. Likely supplies for the Red Coat army. Maybe some Red Coat soldiers, too. Gus, please tell Mr. Adams I would like to confer with him immediately. In the meantime, Mr. Welch, set a course to intercept."

"Aye, Captain," said Augusta.

"Aye, Captain," said Welch.

Johnny saw the six gunports along each side, just as Welch had said. She was smaller than the *Boston*, with no forecastle and a low stern. Her deck rode low against the waves, meaning she was weighted down with something. Guns? Supplies? Men? All three?

Johnny turned to ask Vernon, but he had followed Augusta to the companion hatch. They were going to ask his father what to do. Attack or not?

When Johnny dropped to the hallway, Augusta was there. "Where's Vernon?" asked Johnny.

"Inside your cabin. Your father's finishing shaving."

Johnny pushed open his cabin door and heard, "If there are enemy supplies aboard, Mr. Adams, it is incumbent on us to stop them from reaching American shores. As patriots, it's what we must do!" Vernon's dark eyes were lit with barely-controlled anger.

Johnny's father removed the last bits of shaving cream from his chin and examined the result in the wall mirror. "Johnny," said his father. "What do you think we should do? Attack or not?"

Vernon spoke again before Johnny could answer, "It's a question of honor, Mr. Adams, a question of –"

"I'd like to hear what Johnny thinks," interrupted Johnny's father.

"Have you spoken with Dr. Noel?" asked Johnny.

Vernon interjected again. "What does a French doctor matter? We are an American ship with the chance to stop a British ship from reaching American shores!"

Johnny's father ignored Vernon. "What do you think, Johnny?"

"If there are enemy supplies aboard, we should try to stop them. But Dr. Noel may say there are other things at play."

Johnny's father laughed. "I'm sure he will. But can we win? Can we defeat the ship?"

"Of course," interjected Vernon. "If we can't beat a ship with half the guns we have, why are we here at all?"

"We are here, Mr. Vernon," said Johnny's father. "Because an ocean separates us from our best chance for an ally – France. We are here to convince the French king to send hundreds of ships to help us. We are not here to fight every ship we come across."

An awkward silence filled the room. Johnny's father pulled on his waistcoat. He buttoned it closed. Vernon seethed but kept his mouth shut.

There was one thing his father wanted more than anything else. "Pappa, they may have newspapers aboard," said Johnny.

Johnny's father laughed. "You know exactly what motivates me, don't you, Johnny? Maybe rhetoric is your calling! Let's see what Captain Tucker thinks we should do." Johnny's father put his papers carefully into a weighted sack. "If we don't survive, I want these papers to go to the bottom of the ocean."

Vernon clapped Johnny on the back. "Let's go fight the British, Johnny!"

When they found Captain Tucker on the forecastle, he was arguing with Dr. Noel.

Captain Tucker said, "I will put a guard on the rudder."

"It is not the rudder," said Dr. Noel. "It is that we will lose whether we win or lose."

"What are your thoughts, Mr. Adams?" asked the Captain. "Should we fight or let that British ship go?"

Johnny's father looked at Dr. Noel. "If there are enemy supplies aboard her – guns, ammunition, or soldiers – then American lives will be lost if we let her go."

"Prepare for battle!" shouted the captain.

Dr. Noel shook his head.

With yells and shouts, the sailors flew into action. Cannonballs, rags, and gunpowder rose from the main hold. The gunports came open. The cannons were pulled into place. Jamison's Marines climbed with muskets into the masts.

"Where should the boys go?" asked Johnny's father.

"There's no place absolutely safe in a battle," said Captain Tucker. "If they're in the center of the ship, the gunpowder room could explode. Along the side a cannonball could hit them. Too low and they run the risk of sinking with the ship. The best place is my cabin, but there's danger there, too."

"To the captain's cabin, then, Johnny. And you, too, Vernon and Deane," said Johnny's father.

"But –" started Vernon.

The captain interrupted him. "That's where you'll be, Mr. Vernon. Gus will go with you."

Gus interjected, "But I don't want to watch Vernon."

The captain turned to Gus. "You will watch Vernon. That's an order. Mr. Vernon, any other questions?"

Vernon's shoulders slumped. "No," he said and mumbled something more that no one else could hear.

"Good," said Captain Tucker. "All four of you to my cabin."

Dr. Noel followed them and descended down the companion hatch saying, "*C'est pas bien. C'est pas bien . . .*"

Johnny translated Dr. Noel's words in his head. "This is not good. This is not good . . ."

With the British ship forward of the *Boston*, there was nothing to see in the captain's backward-looking windows. Deane put his face close to the porthole on the side and said, "I still can't see anything!"

Vernon paced the cabin. He muttered. His face turned red. Finally he said, "It's an abomination that I be kept here! I must see that justice is done to the British!"

"Relax, Vernon," said Augusta. "There probably won't even be a fight. We'll chase them down, pass by her, then come around broadside on her bow. The captain will show our guns, and the British ship will strike her colors. There won't be a fight. We'll beat her with seamanship, not guns."

"That's not justice!" raged Vernon. "They must pay!"

Johnny stood at the door listening to the shouts of sailors and officers. The cannons must be loaded now. The Marines must be in their perches. Captain

Tucker and his father must be at the main mast. He opened the door a crack to look out.

Johnny felt a push in his back. "Step aside, Johnny," said Vernon. "I will not be kept away from the fight!" With that, Vernon was gone.

Gus followed. "Where did he go?"

Vernon had already blended in with the sailors on the quarterdeck.

"I don't know," answered Johnny.

"The captain said I should watch him, so I'm going after him!" With that, Gus was gone.

Deane came to the door. It was just the two of them. They looked at each other.

"What should we do, Johnny? Stay here or go after them?"

"The captain told us to stay here," said Johnny

"He told them to stay here, too," said Deane. "And they're gone. Why can't we?"

"I know," said Johnny. "I know, but we were told to stay." He wanted to go. He wanted to see if there would be a battle. If Augusta was right, there would be no danger. Why not go?

"I want to go!" said Deane. "I want to see!"

"Me too," said Johnny. "But we can't. We can't."

Dr. Noel's hulking figure suddenly filled the doorway. "Johnny, your father said you could help me make a hospital, if you will. Please retrieve my medical bag from my room and meet me in the kitchen."

"Yes, of course!" said Johnny.

Deane said, "What about me?"

Dr. Noel sighed. "Yes, Deane, you may help, too."

"Yes!" exclaimed Deane. "Thank you, Dr. Noel!"

Johnny and Deane took the three steps to the companion hatch and dropped down to the hallway. In Dr. Noel's cabin, Johnny moved two books and pulled the medical bag free. "Let's go!"

"Where do you think Vernon went?" asked Deane.

"Don't worry," said Johnny. "Gus will find him."

When they emerged from the companion hatch, the British ship was closer. Much closer. One hundred yards away.

Like Augusta had said they would, the *Boston* was passing by the British ship's side to cross her bow. Johnny's father was at the main mast, standing with Jamison and a Marine. His father aimed a pistol at the British ship. Where was Vernon?

They were almost past the British ship when three puffs of smoke erupted from the British ship.

Johnny heard a strange whistling sound.

Two cannonballs splashed into the *Boston*'s wake.

The third cannonball smashed into the mizzenmast.

The thick wood cracked.

The quarterdeck shook.

Splinters flew everywhere.

"I'm hit!" yelled Deane.

Chapter Eighteen

Johnny dropped the medical bag and rushed to Deane. Deane pulled his sleeves. Two splinters sticking out of his arm. Two tiny red dots formed.

"It's just two small splinters, Deane," said Johnny. "You're fine."

Deane looked down at his arm. "But they really hurt."

"Ready for the turn!" yelled Captain Tucker. "All to the stern!"

Sailors rushed by Johnny. One kicked the medical bag. It slid to the gunwale.

"Go get a bandage below," Johnny told Deane. "I'll get the bag."

"Turn!" yelled Captain Tucker.

The sails dropped as the helmsman made the turn.

There was silence. Every eye was on the British ship. Every ear strained to hear commands. The only sound was water at the *Boston*'s bow.

The sails picked up the new wind, and Captain Tucker ordered, "Ready starboard guns!"

The sailors rushed back from the stern to the guns on the starboard side. Barron repeated the order and lifted his sword above his head. Ten sailors with torches waited. Their heads swiveled between the British ship and Barron's raised sword.

The distance closed to 90 yards. Then 80 yards. Then 70 yards.

"Ready one cannon! One shot across her bow but do not strike her!" shouted the captain. "I will try to save that egg without breaking the shell!"

"One cannon ready!" shouted Barron.

"Fire!" yelled Captain Tucker.

"Fire!" repeated Barron.

Flames shot from a starboard cannon. The deck shook with a boom. Johnny's ears rang.

Johnny saw a splash in the water in front of the British ship, then cannon smoke blocked his view.

The *Boston* turned. For an instant, a gap opened in the smoke. Johnny searched for his father. He was still at the main mast. Still with a pistol pointed at the British ship.

The *Boston* shifted direction again and aimed its bow at the British ship. Barron climbed the short staircase to the foredeck and shouted, "Fore guns at ready!"

On the forecastle, two men poured gunpowder in the cannon's barrel, pushed the cannonball in and shoved in the cloth with a long pole. They lit oil-soaked rags and stood behind the fore gun.

The gap between the two ships widened, but the faster *Boston* turned and made an angle to take the wind across the British ship's bow. As the *Boston* tacked, her starboard guns came into full view of the British ship.

Barron rushed back to the starboard guns and

raised his sword.

"Wait, Mr. Barron," shouted the captain. "Wait!"

Johnny could see the faces of the sailors on the other ship. One of them was racing to the ship's stern.

"Hold . . . hold . . . hold . . ." came the captain's voice.

Vernon suddenly appeared at Johnny's elbow. "Come on!"

"Where's Gus?" asked Johnny, but Vernon had already disappeared into the smoke.

Johnny followed Vernon and found him by the forecastle steps. At the front of the ship, the smoke from the cannon and the burning mizzenmast was gone.

Johnny watched the British ship start. Then her topsails came down. Then her main sails came down. Then her flag dropped.

A cheer rose from the *Boston*.

The British ship had surrendered.

"Hold your fire, men," said Captain Tucker. "But do not let down your guard. We will see if the British keep to their surrender. Mr. Welch, please hail her."

Lieutenant Welch took two striped flags to the starboard deck rail and waved them in a pattern. All the British ship's sails came down. Another cheer came from the *Boston*.

"Leave the foresails up, drop the main sails. Drop the mizzen sails for the turn," shouted Captain Tucker. "All hands to starboard! Prepare to board!"

"Aye, aye," came shouts from everywhere.

Vernon backed away from the gunwale, his face filled with rage.   "What is it?" asked Johnny.

"If the captain will not punish the British, I will! Come on!" said Vernon.

He ran climbed to the forecastle and was swallowed up by smoke and spray as the *Boston* made her turn.

Augusta appeared and tugged on Johnny's arm. "I was afraid of this," she said. "We have to stop him!"

"Stop him from what?" asked Johnny, but Augusta was already gone.

The smoke from the cannon and the burning mizzenmast had settled on the quarterdeck. As the *Boston* slowed to make another turn, the dark mix of ash and gunpowder filled the air. Shouts of "Aye, but I can't see! Turn this way! No – that way!" filled the air.

Everyone was blinded.

Johnny dropped to the deck. He took a deep breath of clean air and looked for Augusta's shoes.

They were next to him. Augusta grabbed Johnny's shoulder. "Come on, what are you waiting for?"

Johnny hesitated. "But –"

"No time!" yelled Augusta. "Come on!" Augusta pushed Johnny forward. Coughing and blinking, Johnny followed Augusta up the stairs to the forecastle.

On the forecastle, the smoke was thick. Johnny waved his arms in the air, but he couldn't see.

Where was Vernon?

Johnny staggered toward where the bow should be and tripped over something.

It was Vernon. He was bent down next to the cannon. "Watch where you're going!" yelled Vernon.

The *Boston* turned. A light breeze carried away some of the smoke. Vernon had the long fuse in the cannon. The lighting pole was under his foot. In his hand was a match, and he was striking it.

Augusta saw it just as Johnny did. "No!" she yelled.

Augusta took two steps at Vernon. She lowered her shoulder to knock him away from the cannon.

Vernon twisted, and Augusta glanced off Vernon's back. She tried to stop, but the slick deck carried her into the railing. She slammed into the hard wood with a sickening crunch.

Augusta groaned.

Vernon laughed and returned to striking his match.

"Vernon, she's hurt!" yelled Johnny, picking himself up off the foredeck.

"She?" asked Vernon. "What she? Hold this pole while I light the end. We're almost on the Britisher."

The *Boston* caught speed with a new wind and turned straight for the British ship. The bow was almost aimed at the Britisher.

"But –" started Johnny as he held the pole. "You can't shoot the British ship, Vernon. They surrendered!"

"Shoot? You mean destroy!" said Vernon. "After what they've done to me – to us – to everyone – they

135

must be punished!"

Vernon struck the match. He lifted it to the oil-soaked pole in Johnny's hand.

Johnny pulled it away. "You can't – you can't do it."

"I can't, Johnny?" sneered Vernon. "I can't?"

Johnny took another step back. Vernon grabbed for the pole, and Johnny backed up again.

"Give it to me!" screamed Vernon, his face twisted in rage.

Johnny glanced around for help. Augusta was groaning at the railing. Everyone was at the stern for the turn. No one could see through the dark smoke on the quarterdeck. No one was near enough to help.

Johnny turned to throw the lit pole into the sea, but he was grabbed by a bony hand.

Vernon's other hand grabbed Johnny's arm and stopped his throw. "What a coward you are! I'll destroy them myself." Vernon yanked the pole from Johnny's hands. He put the match to the oil-soaked end. It flamed to life.

"But they are innocent!" said Johnny.

"My family was too!" answered Vernon. "That did not stop the British from destroying us!"

Vernon stepped toward the cannon.

The *Boston's* bow turned.

In a few seconds, it would point directly at the British ship.

Against the wall, Augusta yelled, "Stop him!"

The world slowed down. The smoke stilled. The

forecastle stopped moving. The wind became a whisper. In a half-second, a hundred thoughts crashed through Johnny's mind and ended with one.

Stop Vernon.

Chapter Nineteen

Vernon was bigger than Johnny. Vernon was faster than Johnny. Vernon was quicker than Johnny.

Vernon had a lit pole in his hands.

Johnny had only his hands.

But Johnny had an idea.

There were ropes. Ropes hanging from the jib boom. And pulleys to lower the sail. He couldn't throw a pulley at Vernon.

What if . . . ?

Johnny pulled a rope from its anchor on the rail.

The *Boston's* bow continued its turn.

Johnny pulled the rope tight. To get the angle, Johnny would have to climb the rail and swing out over the sea. If he timed it just right, Vernon wouldn't see him coming. Maybe his momentum would be enough. Maybe.

The bow completed its turn.

Vernon lowered the burning pole toward the fuse.

Johnny took two quick steps on the rail and leaped over the sea.

He twisted in the air.

There was nothing but sea beneath him.

The rope pulled tight and Johnny flew back toward the ship. His body twisted, and Johnny saw faces on the British ship. Faces of people who would be killed by Vernon's shot.

Johnny lifted his feet to clear the rail.

Vernon put the burning pole to the fuse.

It was too late to hit Vernon.

Johnny adjusted and aimed for the fuse.

He kicked at it as he crossed the cannon. The kick threw Johnny off-balance. He careened into Vernon.

Vernon fell to the deck.

Johnny let go of the rope and slid. His head bounced against the gunwale next to Augusta.

Johnny covered his ears, expecting a boom from the cannon. His fingers came away warm and sticky.

But there was no boom.

Nothing sounded, except a scream from Vernon. "My leg – my leg! Fire! Fire!"

The fuse Johnny kicked out of the cannon had landed on Vernon's cotton breeches.

Vernon furiously swiped at the flame.

Johnny passed out.

Johnny woke up angry.

Where was Vernon?

Johnny scrambled to his elbow, and his head exploded with pain.

He was no longer on the forecastle. There was a ceiling above his head. He smelled baked-in food and cooking oils.

He was in Dr. Noel's makeshift hospital. He was lying on a kitchen table.

Johnny turned to his side.

Vernon looked right back at him.

Johnny jumped.

"Ah, Johnny. Good, you're awake," said Vernon.

Johnny pulled back as far as he could get on the kitchen table.

"I apologize for the misunderstanding on the forecastle," said Vernon quickly.

"What misunderstanding?" asked Johnny.

"It appears you thought I was in some way going to fire on the British ship," said Vernon. "I had no intention of the kind."

"Yes, you did!" said Johnny. "You lit the fuse!"

"I did not intend to," said Vernon. "It was only when you bumped into me that the fuse was lit."

Johnny was confused. He took his mind back to the moments on the forecastle. Grabbing the rope. Swinging out over the sea. Coming back at Vernon.

"It was very dangerous," said Vernon. "You should not have done that. We're very lucky the fore gun did not fire."

"What?" said Johnny. "That's not what—" Johnny shook his head to get it clear. "That's not what happened!"

"It is what happened, Johnny. You think I wanted to fire the fore gun at the British ship?" Vernon laughed. "If I had wanted to do that, I would have done it. But I would never do that."

Johnny turned and stared at the ceiling. Through the planks came the sounds of voices and tramping feet on the quarterdeck. Mr. Griffin's voice boomed, Mr. Welch's followed. Voices responded. A shudder went through the *Boston*.

The British ship was alongside.

"You did do it, Vernon," said Johnny.

Vernon laughed again, less confidently. "If I had meant to fire on the British ship, I would have done it. Did I fire on the British ship? No. If I did not do it, then obviously I did not mean to do it."

"Where is Gus?" asked Johnny.

Vernon's face turned white. "You should be careful, Johnny. Very careful."

With that, Vernon left. On his way out the door, he almost ran into Dr. Noel and Augusta. "Out of my way," said Vernon.

Dr. Noel stood for a moment, then backed away. "Of course, Mr. Vernon."

Augusta didn't move. She stood in the doorway blocking Vernon. "Will you push me away again, Vernon? Like on the forecastle? Will you?"

Vernon glanced at Dr. Noel. "I don't know what you're talking about, boy. As I was explaining to Johnny, there appears to be a misunderstanding. I'll ask you to step out of my way."

Augusta seethed, then smiled. "You'll get what's coming to you Vernon. That's a promise!"

Vernon laughed. "What's coming to me is the return of all that's been taken. So yes, you are right. It will come to me." With that, he pushed past Augusta and was gone.

Dr. Noel entered and examined Johnny. "It was a simple job, yes? Find my medical bag and bring it to me in case anyone was injured, yes? Instead, they bring me you injured and no medical bag."

"I'm sorry, Dr. Noel," said Johnny. "I don't know where your bag is. It was on the quarterdeck, but it was kicked and . . . I don't know what happened to it."

"A sailor brought it to me," said Dr. Noel. "Let me look at you."

Dr. Noel put his large, scarred hands around Johnny's head and turned it side to side and said, "Hrrmph."

"Am I all right?" asked Johnny.

"Yes," said Dr. Noel. "You want scars? Am I so handsome you want to look like me?"

Johnny smiled. "Will I have a scar?"

"No," said Dr. Noel. "You will have to try harder next time. How are you thinking?"

"How am I thinking?" repeated Johnny.

"Yes," said Dr. Noel. "*Tu peux comprendre cette phrase en Francais?*"

"*Oui,*" said Johnny. "I mean, 'Yes.' I can understand that phrase in French."

"Excellent," said Dr. Noel. "I have other problems to attend to."

Augusta found a wet towel and put it to Johnny's head. Her eyes shone with admiration. "You stopped

Vernon!"

"Are you all right?" asked Johnny. "You hit the railing pretty hard."

"I'm fine. Just the wind knocked out of me. But you – you stopped Vernon."

"Vernon says it was a misunderstanding," said Johnny.

"Don't worry," said Augusta. "I'll make sure my father knows what happened."

"Will he believe you? Vernon –"

"You're still not very smart, are you? I'd think after all this, you'd have learned something. You must be adopted after all. At least you're braver than you are smart." Augusta shrugged. "Of course, my father will believe me."

"What will he do?" asked Johnny.

"He'll be angry at Vernon, but Vernon's father is still my father's boss," said Augusta. "There's not much he can do."

"But I –"

"You need to rest. There are new problems now that we are taking many British sailors from the other ship. Dr. Noel wants to talk to you about them when you're better."

Chapter Twenty

Ten days later, Johnny was better. His head wound had healed. His headaches were gone. He wanted to help Mr. Griffin in the masts and get to work.

But Mr. Griffin was gone. With Lieutenant Welch as captain, Mr. Griffin and a skeleton crew had taken command of the British ship. They had turned their bow toward a safe American port. The supplies meant for the British army would instead supply General Washington's troops.

To avoid a mutiny, the British ship's sailors had been taken aboard the *Boston*. They would be deposited in a French port until a trade could be made for American sailors captured by the British. With the ship overflowing, British sailors had been given space on the quarterdeck. Their blankets were spread against both rails on the quarterdeck, cramping movement.

As Johnny stepped gingerly past the British sailors, he heard one say, "John Adams' son." Johnny turned, and British sailor smiled. "Ah, so it's true. You are John Adams' son."

The British sailor's smile showed rotted teeth. His skin had sores like Deane's at the beginning of the journey. Johnny wondered if his wrist was wide where it should be narrow. Did he have rickets?

"Excuse me, boy," said the British sailor. "You'll forgive my curiosity. It's not every day you meet the son of a man the king has sworn to hang."

Johnny rose to his full height. "My father is a champion of liberty. If you are fighting for the British crown, you are fighting against freedom."

"Liberty? Freedom?" scoffed the British sailor. "You have much to learn about this world, boy. There is no liberty, only the power of the strong over the weak."

Augusta suddenly appeared at Johnny's side. "Our free ship just captured your tyrant-owned ship. So which is stronger?"

The British sailor laughed again. "It's just one sea battle and you had more guns than we did and we were loaded down and couldn't maneuver. The war will be the king's. Mark my words!"

Augusta laughed back at the British sailor. "Your king will lose. And you can be sent below in chains rather than be free on the quarterdeck, if you continue to harass our passengers. Would you prefer that removal of freedom?"

"That's a question we were just asking, boy," said the British sailor. "Why aren't we in the main hold? There's room there for us there. Are you hiding something?"

"You can be lashed to the side, if you prefer," said Augusta. "You would slow the ship, but it might be worth it, if it stops us from listening to you."

The British sailor gave a mock bow. "All right, boy. My apologies. Carry on, Master Adams."

"Come on, Johnny," said Augusta. "Let's climb the main mast. I've got something to tell you, if your head is better."

"Let's go," said Johnny.

Augusta led the way. The many weeks aboard the *Boston* had strengthened her arms. She hoisted herself to the first spar, then took two handholds and went to the second. Three more pulls and she was just below the crow's nest. She waved to Johnny. "Come on!"

Since it had been ten days, Johnny went cautiously up the first two handholds. His arms trembled on the lowest spar, but his toes found a firm grip. He lifted with his arms and pushed with his toes and went higher. Looking up, the crow's nest swayed against the sky. Augusta waited impatiently just below it. "Hurry up!" she said.

When Johnny reached Augusta, he stood until his arms stopped shaking.

"Are you all right?" she asked.

"Yes," said Johnny. "It's just been a while."

"While you've been recovering, interesting things have happened," said Augusta. "First, there's Vernon. He's been – Oh, look, he's doing it again!"

Johnny looked down and saw Vernon on the quarterdeck. He was talking to the British sailor with the rotten teeth. "What?" asked Johnny. "What's he doing?"

"Don't you see?" asked Augusta. "He's talking to the British sailors."

"Vernon hates the British. What is he talking to them about?"

"Exactly!" said Augusta. "He's been doing it since they came aboard. Why would Vernon talk to the British? That's the first thing. The second thing is – have you talked to Dr. Noel yet?"

"No – why?"

"He gave me a job to do when we're in port. Maybe he'll give you one, too."

"What job?" asked Johnny.

Augusta paused. "He told me not to tell anyone."

"Does it have anything to do with the spy?"

"He told me not to tell anyone. I wish I could, but I can't. But maybe he'll tell you."

Johnny thought for a moment. What job could it be? What would Dr. Noel have Augusta do in port that she wouldn't do while they're at sea?

"All right," said Johnny. "I'll ask him."

Johnny avoided Deane the rest of the morning and knocked on Dr. Noel's door a few minutes before his French lesson was to start.

Dr. Noel looked from a piece of paper with lines and circles all over it. He quickly put it away and turned to Johnny. "How is your head?"

"It feels good," said Johnny as he closed the door behind him. "What job did you give Gus?"

"What job?" repeated Dr. Noel with a frown. "That was not to be spoken of. I will need to have another talk with Gus."

"What is happening?" asked Johnny. "Can I help?"

"The question is not what is happening, but what will happen," said Dr. Noel. "Have you answered the question of the enemy's greatest strength the way the enemy would answer it?"

Johnny sighed. "Why? Why is it always more questions? Why not answers? It's a simple question that you won't answer. Can I help? I want to help!"

Dr. Noel smiled. "I know, Johnny. I know. But your role in this battle will be different than Gus's. Different than mine. Different, even, than your father's. To be ready for it, you must learn to answer the most important questions yourself."

Johnny shook his head. "I don't even know what that means."

"It means you will be a leader. But a special kind of leader. A leader not like a king. Not like a lord who commands. You will be a leader of individuals animated by a thing which you do not control. It is much harder, but it begins with asking the right questions."

"What do you mean? I don't understand."

Dr. Noel stared at Johnny for a moment. "Perhaps this question will help: What directs a storm?"

"That question doesn't help," said Johnny. "I don't know what directs a storm!"

"A storm comes from the air," said Dr. Noel. "Air around us even now, as we speak. Air that is calm. Air that floats through the world. Then, the air comes together. Under the right circumstances, it becomes a storm. A storm that unleashes a terrible force. A force stronger than any person. A force stronger than a king. But what directs the storm?"

Johnny was frustrated. "I still don't know."

"Exactly," nodded Dr. Noel. "You do not know. No one knows, but there is something. Something that tells the storm when to build. Something that tells the storm where to go. Something that only the air understands. A Sovereign Hand? Or something the Sovereign Hand has created? If you want to direct a storm, you must understand what that thing is. You must know what animates the air."

"What is it?" asked Johnny.

"I told you already: No one knows. Or perhaps a few know. With his experimentations in electricity, maybe Dr. Franklin knows," said Dr. Noel.

"I don't understand. No one knows, but there is something?" asked Johnny.

"Yes. And so it is also with men. There is something that tells men where to go. Something that tells men what to do. Something that tells individuals to act together."

"What is it?" asked Johnny.

Dr. Noel shrugged. "Lords and kings think it is fear. They think punishments and whippings move people. But I and your father and everyone who fights for freedom believe there are different things, good things that bring people together."

"What good things?" asked Johnny.

"Things like rationality and reasonable thinking. Or a loving God. Or a Sovereign Hand. If you believe those things are in every person, then we can live as individuals. We can pursue happiness. We can work together. Live together. Build a new society together. Not because a king or a lord told us to do it. You can trust that good will win. Not fear. Not threats or punishments or whippings. You can trust that good men will come together when needed and become a storm stronger than any king. But if you believe that, you must also believe it is difficult to be a leader of good men. It is like directing a storm. Has your father told you why he writes so many letters to newspapers?"

"Yes," said Johnny. "To persuade others of the justice of our cause."

Dr. Noel nodded. "He is trying to direct the storm. He is trying to give the storm weight and strength and direction."

"What does any of this have to do with the job you gave Gus? Is it about the spy?"

"It does, in a way," said Dr. Noel. "If you believe that something animates us all, then you do not believe we each must wait for orders. We believe that when we act, we do not act alone. We have faith like the air has faith in the air around it. We will act together, though we act as individuals."

Johnny shook his head. "You're not going to tell me the job you gave to Gus, are you?"

Dr. Noel smiled. "No."

"What will happen next?"

Dr. Noel's smile turned to a frown. "I do not know. I believe it was a mistake to take the British ship because now Lord North's spy became more powerful. He has had enough time to find the like-minded among the British sailors."

"Are you certain he stayed with us? Couldn't he have gone with Lieutenant Welch and Mr. Griffin?"

Dr. Noel shook his head. "He is Lord North's spy. Of course he stayed with us."

"What will we do?" asked Johnny.

"We will wait," said Dr. Noel.

"Why must we wait?" asked Johnny. "Isn't there something we can do?"

"What would you have us do?"

"Something," said Johnny. "Anything."

"And tell the spy we know he is here? Then we lose our advantage."

Johnny frowned. "So we wait?"

Deane pushed open the door and walked in. "Hello, Johnny. I didn't know you were back. How are you feeling?"

Dr. Noel ignored Deane and said, "We wait."

Chapter Twenty-One

The next day, Johnny waited on the quarterdeck.

He waited to know what to do. If he was like the air, he was waiting for something to tell him to join the storm.

But what would tell him? Would the spy do something? Would someone else do something? Johnny didn't know. But he was doing what Dr. Noel said to do: Waiting.

Deane bounced up to Johnny. "Want to try Hazard again for the rubber ball? It was too dank in the doldrums to go where the sailors are, and then there was the storm and the battle with the British ship. And I wanted to do it with you, so I haven't tried again. Will you go with me?"

"Do you know what to do this time?" asked Johnny.

"Yes," said Deane. "I double checked with Gus. I should have the sailor with the ball choose the main and throw the dice."

"All right," said Johnny. "Let's go."

When they went below the waterline, the stench was awful. It was like the captain's flour shower and washing had not been done at all. Johnny's stomach didn't revolt like the first time, but he held his nose just in case.

As soon as the sailors saw Deane, they circled around. There were fewer faces since some had gone with Mr. Griffin, but the black sideburned sailor was there. "What have you to bet this time, Mr. Deane?"

"A leather belt with a silver belt buckle," said Deane.

An approving murmur went through the sailors. "All right," said the sideburned sailor. "Three to one odds will be fair."

"But this time, you choose the main," said Deane. "And you roll the dice."

The sailors groaned. "It's all right, boys," said the sailor. "It's all right. I agree to Mr. Deane's terms. As my main, I choose 7. Mr. Deane, hand over the belt so it's here in the middle. Clear a space, men, so I can roll."

Deane took off his belt and kept one hand holding up his pants. The sailors cleared a space.

The sailor threw the dice.

They came up three and four.

Seven.

"Oh no," groaned Deane.

"Bad luck for you Mr. Deane," said the sailor. "But you have two more chances. Here's my second roll."

The dice came up three and four again.

Another seven.

"Are you cheating again?" thundered Deane. "That's impossible to get the same numbers twice!"

153

The sideburned sailor turned to the other sailors. "Did Mr. Deane call me a cheater? Did he? Did you Mr. Deane?"

Deane cowered. "No, I didn't. But it's awful strange that you got the same numbers twice."

Johnny stepped in. "Since you say you aren't cheating, let Deane throw the last roll."

A murmur went through the sailors. "That's highly irregular in Hazard," said the sideburned sailor. "But I'll agree to your terms. If Deane rolls a seven, he wins. Dekker, hand him the dice."

A sailor handed dice to Deane.

Deane cradled them in his hand, blew on them, and rolled them across the floor.

They came up a one and a two.

"Ah, so sorry, Mr. Deane," said the sideburned sailor. "The belt is mine."

"How —" started Johnny. "Were those the same dice?"

"Now, you're saying I was cheating, Mr. Adams?" said the sideburned sailor. "I won fair and square. Come back if you have anything else silver to gamble."

Deane huffed back up the stairs with a hand on his pants. "Johnny, what do I do? I don't have another belt."

"I don't have an extra," said Johnny. "Let's see if we can get some rope."

Just as they arrived on the quarterdeck, a sailor shouted from the crow's nest. "Land, ho!"

It was followed by another shout. "Ship coming toward us, Captain!"

Captain Tucker yelled back, "Is she friendly?"

"She's putting up signaling flags, Captain," said the sailor in the crow's nest.

A moment passed. "She says, 'Welcome,' Captain," said a sailor in the top mast. "And she's under a French flag. A French ship!"

"Mr. Barron, thank them with a shot of the fore gun, if you please!"

"Aye, aye, Captain," said Mr. Barron. He and two sailors went to the forecastle.

Seconds later, there was an explosion and smoke and screams.

The captain rushed past Johnny. "Johnny, get Dr. Noel!"

When Johnny brought Dr. Noel to the forecastle, Barron's leg was in tatters. His blood was everywhere. A shard of iron from the cannon had gone through it. Cannon pieces were all over the forecastle.

Dr. Noel examined Barron quickly and ordered him taken to the kitchen.

"What happened?" asked Johnny.

"We loaded it like always," said a stunned sailor. "But it exploded."

An hour later, Johnny entered Dr. Noel's cabin. Laid out on the floor were pieces of the exploded cannon. Dr. Noel pointed to the thickest part. "You see, Johnny, it exploded there. Someone overloaded the cannon with gunpowder. This was done on

155

purpose."

"Lord North's spy?" asked Johnny.

"Most likely," answered Dr. Noel. "You know what else this means? You saved Vernon's life when he tried to light it."

Johnny took it all in. "But that means the spy –"

"Yes," said Dr. Noel. "I feared something like this when we attacked the British ship."

"And now Lord North's spy has the British sailors as reinforcements," said Johnny.

"Yes, yes, he does," said Dr. Noel. "He will feel more powerful. He will feel like he can do something. Which means we should give him something to do."

"What? What will we give him to do?" asked Johnny.

Dr. Noel took a long hard look at Johnny. "Have you answered the question of the enemy's greatest strength? If so, you will know what the spy is doing, and you will know what we are doing."

Johnny shook his head. "I don't know . . . I don't know!"

"Think about it the way they would," said Dr. Noel. "Put yourself in their place. In their heads. Then you will find the answer."

"Tell me the answer!" exclaimed Johnny. "If you do, I can help now!"

Dr. Noel paused to consider. "You would be a help. And you will be a help. But not yet. Now, I must go check on Mr. Barron."

An hour later, Dr. Noel rose to the quarterdeck in

a blood-stained apron and found Captain Tucker at the wheel. "We did all we could, Captain," said Dr. Noel. "The arterial damage was too great to save him."

Captain Tucker was silent for a moment. "Mr. Barron was a good man. A good sailor. Such a shame to lose him. We'll have a service at sunset and bury him at sea. Will you tell your father, Johnny?"

"Yes, captain," said Johnny. "Of course."

"Such a shame," repeated Captain Tucker. "Such a shame."

At sunset, everyone gathered on the quarterdeck around Mr. Barron's wrapped body. It was lying on a plank. Pieces of the cannon that had killed him were tied to his ankles as weights.

Even the British sailors were quiet and respectful while the captain read passages from the Bible.

When the service was over, Mr. Barron's body was lifted by four sailors and taken to the rail.

At a word from Captain Tucker, the plank was tilted.

Mr. Barron's body fell into the sea.

The sailors returned to their work, more subdued than usual. Barron's death dropped a pall over the ship. The British sailors stayed out of the way of the American sailors.

Few words were spoken at dinner in the captain's cabin. Lieutenant Barron had been well-liked by everyone. Now, he was gone.

After dinner, Johnny heard hushed words between

Captain Tucker and Dr. Noel. He couldn't hear what they said, but he saw that Captain Tucker was at first angry, then incredulous, then resigned to what Dr. Noel was saying.

The next day, Johnny found Augusta and Deane and Captain Tucker on the forecastle. Captain Tucker was naming the many types of ships along the coast. "You see the smaller ships? Those are single-masted galleons for fishing. Those two-masted ships are sloops, and they're for taking goods from France to Spain and back again. There is a three-masted ship like ours, setting sail for America or the West Indies. When this war is over, the *Boston* will be one of them."

"You'll take goods across the ocean?" asked Johnny.

"Yes, indeed," said Captain Tucker. "I expect to make my fortune by my fifth voyage, if no cannons explode and kill me along the way. If I survive the voyages, there will be enough money to take the rest of my life to spend. Enough for my family to take the rest of their lives to spend." He winked at Gus too quickly for Deane to see, then pointed toward the coast. "There's a corvette with its guns out. To keep pirates away. In the service of the Spanish king, I think."

Deane pointed at a ship behind them. "What kind of ship is that, Captain?"

Captain Tucker took out his eyeglass. "It has a French flag, but it's built in the British way. It may be a British ship captured by a French captain in the Indies. But with all that's happened so far, we should keep an eye on it. Johnny, will you take a watch? Go up the topmast and see what it does for the next hour? I'll order some changes in course and see if she follows."

"Aye, aye, Captain!" said Johnny.

In ten seconds, Johnny had climbed up the topmast. He stood in the crow's nest and shielded his eyes against the western sun. Below, orders were given to change course.

The ship in the distance kept its course. It didn't turn.

Johnny watched for thirty minutes. It didn't seem to follow the *Boston*.

The captain had said to watch it for an hour, so Johnny stayed in the crow's nest. His mind wandered again to the questions Dr. Noel had asked.

Dr. Noel said he had them backward. He said the first question to answer was "What is the enemy's greatest strength?"

England's greatest strength wasn't its army. American soldiers had defeated them several times since Bunker Hill. General Washington had surprised them crossing the Delaware on Christmas a year before. Then, there was the victory at Saratoga, where the English General Burgoyne surrendered. The British army wasn't the enemy's greatest strength.

England's greatest strength was its ships. England's ships did everything important for the British crown.

They ferried soldiers from city to city. They supplied them. They blockaded the American coast so American ships couldn't trade with Europe. The enemy's greatest strength was its ships.

What was the next question Dr. Noel said he should ask?

It was about fear. What was the enemy's greatest fear?

Johnny tried to put himself in the place of King George. In the place of Lord North. What did they fear?

Nothing, thought Johnny.

If he were as powerful as the English, he would fear nothing.

They were the most powerful force on earth. More powerful than the colonists. More powerful than France. More powerful than anyone else in Europe.

What could they fear?

Johnny looked again, and the ship behind them had made a turn.

A turn toward the *Boston*.

Was it following them?

Johnny dropped down to the quarterdeck and found Captain Tucker standing with Dr. Noel on the stern.

"It followed us, Captain Tucker," reported Johnny. "It turned to follow our course."

Dr. Noel grimaced. "I do not think that is a French ship. Despite its flag."

"The British have found us again?" asked Johnny.

"Perhaps," said Captain Tucker. "But I do not think they will do anything in these waters."

"Yes," said Dr. Noel. "But Lord North's spy will have seen them, too."

"What does that mean?" asked Johnny. "Does that mean he will do something?"

"Not now," said Dr. Noel. "But perhaps soon. In Bordeaux."

Dr. Noel took a long look at the ship in the distance and turned to Johnny. "If you will help me now, I will use it."

Chapter Twenty-Two

"Of course I will help," said Johnny. "Of course! What can I do? What is it?"

"Perhaps not," said Dr. Noel. "You are too eager."

"I'm – I'm sorry, Dr. Noel." Johnny took a deep breath. "I won't be so eager. What do you want me to do?"

Dr. Noel looked long at Johnny. "First, have you answered the question of greatest strength the way the British would answer it?"

"Yes. The greatest strength of the British, they think, is their ships."

"Good," said Dr. Noel. "And what does that mean for the second question? What is their greatest fear?"

"I don't know," said Johnny.

"No ideas?" asked Dr. Noel.

"I don't think they fear anything. I wouldn't, if I had as many big ships as they do."

"Think again," said Dr. Noel. "The answer to the second question comes from the answer to the first."

The enemy's fear came from their strength? Johnny thought as hard as he could.

"Their greatest fear . . ." started Johnny. "Is it that something would happen to their ships? That someone would take away their ships? That their ships would be threatened?"

"Yes, Johnny. You have answered the second question. The enemy's greatest fear is that someone would take away their greatest strength. That something would stop their ships."

Johnny was disappointed. "But everyone knows that. That's why we're sailing to France. So the French king will give us ships to fight against the British ships."

Dr. Noel smiled. "That is what appears on the surface, Johnny. But think deeper. Is there another way to stop the British ships?"

Johnny tried to think deeper, but he didn't know how. What did that even mean?

Dr. Noel smiled. "Several years ago, a student at Yale tried to think deeper about the problem. He knew the British thought of their ships as their strength and their greatest fear was something that would stop them. He wondered what he could do. He thought long and deep and hard about that question."

"What did he do? Build cannons?"

"No," said Dr. Noel.

"Build a bigger ship?" asked Johnny.

"No," said Dr. Noel.

"Get ships from somewhere else?"

"No," said Dr. Noel.

"Then how?" asked Johnny.

"I think you will discover the answer yourself with enough time," said Dr. Noel.

Johnny let out a sigh. He had to wait again! Why

could Dr. Noel never just answer a question?

"But," continued Dr. Noel. "We do not have the time. I will tell you what happened."

"Finally!" said Johnny.

"What do you mean – finally?" asked Dr. Noel.

"Nothing. I'm sorry," said Johnny. "Please go ahead."

Dr. Noel nodded. "This Yale student was named David Bushnell. He started by experimenting with making gunpowder explode under water. As you know, gunpowder does not fire when wet, so this was a difficult problem. He found if he encased it properly and set a flint, he could set these 'mines' in the water to attack the British ships. But there was a problem."

"What problem?" asked Johnny.

"There was no way to put the mine against the British ships. The British ships kept guards at all times. They kept an eye out for boats slipping up next to their ships. And if they saw a boat get too close, they would shoot at it. If the boat had mines in it, it would blow up and kill everyone on the boat. So Bushnell had a new problem to solve. He had a new question to answer: How do you get close to the British ships without them knowing you were there?"

"How?" asked Johnny. "He answered it? How?"

"Underwater," said Dr. Noel.

"Underwater? But how?"

"With something Bushnell called the *Turtle*. Or *tortue* in French."

"He strapped gunpowder to a turtle?"

"Not a turtle, Johnny. the *Turtle*. A small craft that could go underwater. It held one man and could carry 150 pounds of gunpowder to set against the side of a British ship."

"It wasn't a real turtle? Why did Bushnell call it the *Turtle*?"

"Because it looks like two halves of a turtle shell stuck together. It's narrow in the front, then bulges out in the middle, then narrow in the back. With three corkscrews. One in front, one in back, and one on top."

"How did it go underwater?" asked Johnny.

"There was a small hatch on top with glass for the operator to use. He could see out of it, but he could also close it and go deep. Underwater, he used the three corkscrews by foot and by arms to propel him and steer."

Johnny got excited. "And it worked? Why haven't I heard of it? Why aren't we using it against the British ships?"

"Because it didn't work," said Dr. Noel. "It didn't work as it should. When they tried it against General Howe's ship in New York Harbor, the tide was stronger than the corkscrews and the operator had to tread water for five hours. When he got to General Howe's ship, he couldn't attach the mine to it. The British saw him and chased him, but he got away. That was closest the *Turtle* came to working. It never worked again."

Johnny's head was spinning. "So that's – that's

what the British fear most? The *Turtle*?"

Dr. Noel nodded. "If your ships were your greatest strength, wouldn't you fear something that could destroy them without any way for you to defend against it?"

Johnny's spinning head came to a sudden stop. "What does that have to do with us?"

Dr. Noel looked closely at Johnny. "If you had a problem with a new invention that could win a war, what would you do?"

"I'd get help," answered Johnny.

"From whom?" asked Dr. Noel. "If you could get help from anyone in the world, who would you go to?"

"A great inventor."

"And who is the greatest inventor of our age?" asked Dr. Noel.

"Dr. Franklin, of course! Benjamin Franklin!" exclaimed Johnny.

"Exactly," said Dr. Noel. "Dr. Franklin. Lord North's spy discovered our secret purpose, but I do not think he discovered everything."

"Secret purpose?" repeated Johnny.

"Of course," said Dr. Noel. "We are taking Bushnell's plans of the *Turtle* to Dr. Franklin, to see if he can fix it."

Johnny was stunned. "Those were the secret plans I heard the spy talking about? Bushnell's plans of the *Turtle*?"

Dr. Noel nodded. "Lord North's spy knows we

have the *Turtle* plans aboard this ship. That is his purpose: to steal those plans for Lord North. It is also why I did not think he would act unless he could get away. He would be worried we would throw the plans overboard and they would be lost."

"And now?" asked Johnny. "Now that we are in Bordeaux? What will he do?"

"There are seven things the spy could do. For five of them, you are not needed. For the two in which you are needed, one will happen on the ship. The other will happen in Bordeaux. For the thing on the ship, you must divert attention. For the thing in Bordeaux, you must have quick hands and be a thief. I will tell you what to do when the time comes. Can you be ready to do those things but not too eager? If you are too eager, Lord North's spy will see it. If you are too eager, he will expect what will happen."

"Yes," said Johnny, even though he had never diverted attention or used quick hands to be a thief.

If Dr. Noel thought he could do it, he would do it.

"I will be ready."

Chapter Twenty-Three

At a bend in the river, Bordeaux appeared. From a distance, it looked like Boston. Buildings clustered near the water with rolling hills behind. Church spires stretched to the sky. Along the docks, workers teemed between warehouses and a wide loading area.

As they sailed closer, it looked nothing like Boston. The embankments were stone, not wood. The workers wore strange loose clothing that ballooned at their legs. The churches were bigger than anything in Boston. Bigger than any building Johnny had ever seen. And the water wasn't dark blue. It was brown.

Captain Tucker dropped the anchor between two French merchant ships. One of the French ships sent an invitation to dinner.

"Finally, I will get some news!" exclaimed Johnny's father. "Let's see what has happened in France these last months while we've been at sea. And they may have news of events in Britain and America, too. We've been gone so long. Johnny, would you like to come?"

Johnny remembered what Dr. Noel had said about needing help. "No, thank you, Pappa. I'll stay on the *Boston*. But Vernon would probably like to go."

"All right, son. I'll take Vernon. Don't get into trouble while I'm gone."

"Yes, Pappa," said Johnny.

Johnny went to the quarterdeck and found Dr. Noel had declined the French captain's invitation, too. It was strange for someone who missed French food so much. Strange enough that Johnny suspected one of the seven things might happen soon. Maybe the one that Johnny could help with. Maybe the one where Johnny would create a diversion.

But Dr. Noel didn't say anything more to Johnny. Johnny stood near him for a while, then decided to climb the main mast for a better view of Bordeaux.

The port's din dropped to a gentle hum as darkness settled. Dockworkers stored the day's last barrels and crates. Lanterns were lit. Shouts gave way to laughter, as the evening's first revelers arrived. A mist rose from the river. The last light faded on the cathedral's spires.

Johnny enjoyed the gentle sway of the main mast and the comfortable breeze. He kept an eye on Dr. Noel. Below, two Marines watched the British sailors. All the rest of the crew, it seemed, was below deck, packing things for shore.

Captain Tucker led Dr. Noel and Augusta to the forecastle and pointed to something on the docks. Johnny couldn't make out what they were looking at. The mist made it hard to see.

Johnny was about to climb down when Augusta left. She went from the forecastle past the milling British sailors with a nod to the Marines.

Before Johnny could drop to the quarterdeck and

join her, two things happened.

Two things happened with military precision.

The first thing was the British sailors threw off their chains. Chains that should have been locked. Chains that should have held the British sailors in place.

But they weren't locked.

They didn't hold the British sailors in place.

Before the Marines could call for help, rags went in their mouths. The British sailors stripped the muskets from the Marines. They pulled the Marines' hands behind their backs and held them tight.

Then, the second thing happened.

A handful of British sailors rushed to the forecastle.

Their leader called out, "Captain Tucker, do not shout for help."

Captain Tucker spun around.

"We have your cabin boy, Captain Tucker. We'll slit his throat, if I'm not listened to."

Behind the British sailors, Augusta had a knife against her back. She was being forced to the rear of the ship.

Captain Tucker's face turned crimson. "What – is – the – meaning –of – this?"

The British leader threw up his hands. "Just a few things we'd like to discuss before we're on French soil."

"This is a violation of the laws of the sea and the rules of –" started Captain Tucker.

"Please, please," interrupted the British leader. "It'll just be a moment. Come down, and we'll talk."

Instead, Captain Tucker pulled a pistol from his waistband. He pointed it at the British leader. "Release my cabin boy!"

The British leader put his hands in the air again. "Shooting British sailors in a French port will not be good, I think," he said. "But if you can't listen for a minute . . . by all means, shoot me. My friends will overwhelm you. You'll die, your cabin boy will die. I don't know what happens after that. A high price to pay for an exchange of words."

Captain Tucker looked at Dr. Noel.

Dr. Noel nodded.

Captain Tucker's pistol dropped. "Say what you have to say."

The British sailor stepped forward and started talking quietly to Captain Tucker.

At the other end of the ship, there was a sharp scream as two British sailors forced Augusta into the Captain's cabin.

Suddenly, Johnny understood.

The British sailors weren't talking to the captain for any reason.

It was a diversion.

But it wasn't a diversion Dr. Noel had created.

It was a diversion the British sailors had created.

The British wanted something from the Captain's cabin, and they were diverting the Captain's attention while they took it.

The *Turtle* plans. It had to be.

In the strongbox. In the Captain's cabin.

And Augusta had they key.

Johnny opened his mouth to yell. To warn the sailors below. To sound the alarm.

But his voice wouldn't be enough. They wouldn't hear him below the quarterdeck. If he yelled, it would only alert the British sailors. They would climb the mast and grab him.

Johnny looked back to the Captain on the forecastle. Next to him was Dr. Noel. Dr. Noel was looking at him.

Johnny motioned with his hands toward the captain's cabin, but Dr. Noel didn't respond.

The mist thickened, and Dr. Noel's face was obscured.

Johnny didn't know what to do.

Johnny looked again, but Dr. Noel had turned away.

Johnny didn't know what Dr. Noel was trying to say.

It didn't matter.

Johnny was the only one who could see what was happening. He was the only one who had seen both the British sailors get free of their chains and Gus get ushered into the captain's cabin.

He was the only one who had seen what was happening.

He was the only who could do something.

But what?

Yelling wouldn't help because the crew below wouldn't hear him.

But they would hear the bell.

If he reached the bell, he could ring it. He could sound the alarm. American sailors would overpower the British sailors.

If he reached the bell.

But the bell was at the back of the ship. He was in the main mast near the front of the ship. The British sailors were in-between. Johnny couldn't drop down without them seeing. But . . . Johnny's eyes went up.

Could he? Dare he?

Most ropes had been stowed for port, but two were still tied at the tops of the mast. If he freed one and used it to swing, he could get to the mizzenmast. If he got to the mizzenmast, he could drop to the bell.

Johnny calculated what it would take.

If he ran along the port-side spar just below the crow's nest, there was a chance. He'd have to jump. As he was swinging, he would need to slide down the rope. If he did it just right, he could land on the mizzenmast. From there, he could drop to the bell.

But it had to be done quietly.

If the British sailors heard him, they would grab him before he rang the bell. It had to be done quietly or it would be for nothing.

Johnny pulled the bottom of the rope free. He tugged to be sure the knot at the top held. He took a deep breath and ran along the spar.

One step. Two steps.

On the third, Johnny jumped into the air.

He swung over the British sailors. Over the hatches. Over the quarterdeck.

Johnny slipped down the rope and reached for the rolled-up canvas on the mizzenmast.

It was wet from the harbor mist. Johnny's fingernails scratched against the surface but found no seam. He couldn't find a grip.

The rope had reached its zenith. Now, it was pulling him back.

Johnny grabbed the rope with two hands and turned to see he was going straight at the main mast.

At the last second, Johnny shifted his weight and turned in midair. He kicked off the spar and missed the main mast by inches.

The rope wrapped around the main mast in tighter circles. He braced himself and bumped against the hard wood with a quiet thud.

Johnny looked down.

Had they heard him?

No one looked up.

Time to try again.

Johnny unwrapped the rope, pulled it tight and ran.

One step. Two steps. Faster on the third step.

Johnny jumped into the air.

When his swing reached its peak, Johnny let go of the rope. He slammed into the wet canvas and grabbed at it with both hands.

His hands found a grip on the slippery canvas.

He pulled his legs over and held on tight.

The empty rope swung back to the main mast. It hit with a tiny thwack.

British heads looked up.

But they looked at the main mast.

Johnny hid behind the furled sail.

After a count of ten, Johnny poked an eye out and saw the tops of British heads. No faces turned up.

Johnny inched to the mizzenmast and loosened a rope. He lowered it until the end hung just above the deck. He tied a knot around the mizzenmast spar and slid down the rope.

Johnny dropped silently to the quarterdeck.

The bell was just a few steps away.

Johnny tiptoed to it. He grabbed the hammer and pulled it high.

"Ring that bell, the boy dies," said a whisper from the darkness.

Augusta was pushed forward by two sailors. One was dressed like an American. It was the sailor who had given the dice to Deane below. What had the sideburned sailor called him? Dekker?

The other man was a British sailor. He held a knife in Augusta's back.

Augusta shook her head sideways. The way Dr. Noel had done just a minute before.

What did she mean?

"Don't do it, boy," said Dekker. "Don't ring that bell."

175

Johnny's arm stayed raised. All he had to do was hit the bell, and the crew would come.

But what about Augusta?

Dekker inched toward Johnny.

A bell sounded across the water. A church bell in Bordeaux.

Johnny turned at the sound, and Dekker grabbed Johnny's upraised arm.

"That's it, boy," said Dekker with a chuckle, taking the hammer from Johnny's hand. "Easy now."

"Who are you?" asked Johnny.

"I go by Dekker on this ship, but I have many names." He pushed Johnny toward the British sailor, who grabbed Johnny by the shoulder and squeezed him against Augusta.

"The boat should be here," said the British sailor.

"Who are you?" asked Johnny, trying desperately to buy time. "I don't understand."

Dekker looked sideways at Johnny, a malicious look on his face and a slight tremor in his voice. "It doesn't matter who I am."

And Johnny knew. He recognized the voice.

Dekker had severed the rudder in the doldrums.

Dekker put the letter in the dead sailor's pocket.

Dekker put too much gunpowder in the fore gun.

It was Dekker who Johnny heard the first night on the ship.

It was Dekker who unlocked the chains of the British sailors.

Dekker was Lord North's spy.

Then, the companion hatch stirred between them. They both took a step back. The lid came up.

Out came Deane's head.

"Johnny, I finally won! I made them switch the dice each time, and I won! I got a ball to play with!"

"Oh, no," said Augusta.

"Oh, no," said Johnny.

Lord North's spy laughed and said, "Mr. Deane, please come with me."

Chapter Twenty-Four

"Go away, Deane," said Johnny. "We'll play later."

"Let's play now!" said Deane. "If we lose the ball over the side, we'll find it because we're anchored. Right? I think it floats."

"Come a little closer," said Dekker. "Let me see the ball."

"Do you know how to play?" asked Deane.

"Go away, Deane!" said Johnny.

"Why?"

But Dekker was already close enough to grab Deane.

In an instant, Dekker had Deane.

He put a knife to Deane's throat.

"What is happening?" Deane choked.

"Lord North will pay a nice fee for a boy whose father is buying weapons in Paris," said the spy. "Maybe Lord North will pay by the pound."

"What? What is happening?" asked Deane.

"Do I have to explain what a knife means, boy?" sneered Dekker.

"Don't take Deane," said Johnny. "Take me. I won't struggle. Leave Deane here, please."

"Sorry," said the spy. "Young Deane will make me a rich man. And don't think of yelling to the captain.

If you do, Deane will die here."

Deane started to cry.

"Stop blubbering, boy," said the spy. "You won't be harmed if you come nicely."

Deane didn't move. "I don't want to go!"

The spy pressed his knife until it made a red line on Deane's neck.

"Ouch! I'll go. I'll go!" said Deane.

"Take me instead, please!" said Johnny.

"Quiet, boy. Or else!" Lord North's spy stuffed a rag in Deane's mouth. He pushed Deane to the gunwale and forced him over the side.

Johnny wondered: Where was the crew? Where was Captain Tucker? Where was Dr. Noel?

Augusta nudged Johnny and gave a quick nod.

What did she mean?

Augusta raised the sailor's hand to her mouth and bit. At the same time, she stomped on his feet.

"Awww!" howled the British sailor. He put both hands on Augusta.

Johnny was free.

Oh, thought Johnny. That's what she meant.

Johnny ran to the bell.

Before he could get there, two British sailors appeared.

They blocked the way.

Johnny skidded to a stop. He took a step back.

One sailor reached for him. Johnny turned and ran.

Augusta was struggling with her captor. She saw

Johnny running toward them and ducked to turn the sailor's back to Johnny. Johnny lowered his shoulder and slammed into the sailor. Off balance, he fell.

Augusta was free.

She yelled, "Father!" and followed Johnny.

They jumped on the gunwale and ran along its slippery edge.

The British sailors chased after them.

In the water below, the spy's boat pushed away from the ship.

Deane's hands struggled with the tight gag in his mouth, trying to pull it out.

"Yeeelp!" Deane cried.

But Johnny couldn't help. British sailors were on Johnny and Augusta's heels.

"Father!" yelled Augusta again.

Ahead of Johnny, British sailors appeared. He jumped off the gunwale and sprinted back to the bell. Johnny grabbed the hammer and swung with all his might.

The bell sounded.

From below came a murmur. Then a scramble. Then the thunder of climbing feet.

American sailors burst through the hatch.

The British sailors turned to fight the rising American sailors. They beat the first back. But more came. The American sailors punched and kicked their way to the deck, and more followed.

It was a melee on the deck.

"Come on, Johnny!" waved Augusta. "We need to

get Deane!"

She ran at the rope that Johnny had left hanging from the mizzenmast spar. She jumped and started climbing.

Johnny grabbed the bottom of the rope. As he ran, he twisted one of the rope's ends and looped it through, pulling it into knot. He jumped off the gunwale and stood on the knot. With his hands, he held the other end of the rope.

His momentum took the rope and Augusta out over the river.

Deane looked up. Again, he cried, "Yeeelp!"

"Deane, jump out of the boat!" yelled Johnny.

Deane looked up and nodded. But he didn't jump.

Instead, Deane fell backward into the water with a splash.

Back on the gunwale, a British sailor had separated from the melee. He stood with a knife, waiting for Johnny to swing back.

"Climb, Johnny!" screamed Augusta.

Johnny climbed.

Hand over hand.

As fast as he could.

Every last bit of strength.

Johnny looked down and felt a brush against his foot. The brush of a knife blade on his boot.

But Johnny was too high.

When he climbed on the mizzenmast spar, Augusta was already there.

Johnny heard a curse and a British sailor say, "To

the mizzenmast. Let's climb."

Deane was splashing around in the water with the gag in his mouth, yelling, "Yeeeeelp!"

"Gus," said Johnny. "Throw one end of the rope to Deane. We'll pull him up."

Augusta threw the rope to Deane.

Lord North's spy was yelling at Deane, trying to find him in the mist.

Deane grabbed the rope just as the British sailors reached the spar.

"Pull!" said Johnny.

Augusta and Johnny pulled on the rope.

But Deane barely popped out of the water and fell back in.

Deane was too heavy.

"Come on," yelled Augusta. "We need to jump!"

Augusta took her part of the rope and jumped off the spar.

The slack tightened and pulled Johnny off the spar, too.

Johnny fell.

The combined weight of Johnny and Augusta was enough to pull Deane out of the water.

Deane flew up as Johnny and August went down.

They met halfway in a tangle of arms and legs.

"Ow!" yelled Augusta with Deane's elbow in her stomach. "That hurts!"

Johnny was above her on the rope, with Deane below Augusta. He had his arm through a loop in the rope and spun wildly.

Deane's momentum carried the three back toward the ship. Deane grabbed the gunwale with one hand. With the other hand, he held the rope.

Then, their weight pulled them back to the water.

Deane held the rope for a second. Then, two seconds.

Johnny saw what was going to happen.

"Don't let go of the rope, Deane!"

But Deane let go.

Deane's end of the rope snaked up and over the spar.

Johnny and Augusta fell.

On the way down, Augusta yelled, "I can't swim!"

Chapter Twenty-Five

As he fell in the mist, Johnny didn't know where the water was.

How long would it take to hit the water?

A second? Two seconds?

Johnny tucked into a ball.

He hit the surface and sank into thick muddy water.

Opening his eyes, he couldn't see anything. He floated to find which way was up. He kicked. Something splashed beside him. He broke through the surface.

A wooden oar smashed next to him. It lifted and hit the water again. Johnny dove to avoid it.

He stayed down and counted to five. Then he kicked up again.

Something brushed against his arm. He pulled away, thinking it was a fish.

Suddenly, he remembered Augusta. She wasn't on the surface.

Johnny dove again. He dove deep. He spread his arms and legs wide. He turned in circles, wider and wider. Just when he was out of breath, he felt something against his boot.

Johnny dove deeper and reached out. He felt an

arm, found a hand, and grabbed it. His lungs bursting, Johnny kicked to the surface.

He pulled Gus to the air.

She wasn't moving. There was blood on her scalp.

The spy's oar had found her.

Johnny held her in front of him and shook her shoulders.

Her eyes fluttered. She took in a huge breath and pushed Johnny away, but Johnny held on to her shirt.

"What are you doing?" she asked.

"You were knocked out by the oar," said Johnny. "I rescued you from under the water."

"Rescued me?" repeated Augusta. "I'm fine. Ow. My head hurts. Let go of me."

Johnny let go of her shirt, and Augusta started to sink. She flailed her arms wide.

"Don't let go of me!" said Augusta. "Get me to the ship."

Disembodied laughter came over the water. "You found the cabin boy, Johnny," said the spy. "I thought my oar had done enough. No matter. I have what I came for. I have the plans. There's nothing you can do about that. Lord North sends his regards!"

Johnny kicked to the ship. A rope fell in the water next to him. He tied it under Augusta's arms and tugged. The rope went up and pulled Augusta over the rail.

The rope came down again, and Johnny grabbed the top of a knot. He was pulled up faster than he had fallen. He tumbled over the rail to the deck.

Dr. Noel was examining Augusta. Captain Tucker cradled her head in his arms. Deane ripped his wet shirt and offered a piece as a rag for Augusta's head.

Behind them, the Marines had their guns pointed at the British sailors. The British sailors were tied up and back in chains.

Captain Tucker stood up and gave an order. "Cannons out. Point them where you last saw that skiff. Ready to fire on my command!"

The sailors jumped into action. They rolled the cannons forward. Loaded the gunpowder. Stuffed the ball and tamped it down. They lit the sticks.

Dr. Noel rose. "Captain, no! You must not!"

Captain Tucker turned to Dr. Noel. "They are still in range, Doctor."

"You cannot shoot cannons in the middle of a French port. If you do, the fort will take it as an attack. They will blow this ship to pieces."

Captain Tucker slapped the gunwale with frustration. "You are right, Doctor. Gentlemen, stand down. Disarm and unload the cannons."

"But Dr. Noel," said Johnny. "The plans! He has the plans!"

"What plans?" asked Deane.

Captain Tucker cut them off. "Gentlemen! To my cabin, please."

Johnny and Deane followed Captain Tucker to his cabin. At the cabin door, Captain Tucker stopped. "Mr. Deane, would you gather dry clothes for Johnny?"

"Of course," said Deane.

Dr. Noel pushed past them with Augusta in his massive arms.

"Come on in, Johnny. Much to discuss."

Inside, Augusta held a piece of Deane's shirt to her head. Dr. Noel was next to her smiling.

Captain Tucker smiled broadly, too. "Well done, Dr. Noel! Well done!"

"Thank you, Captain, but it was Gus who deserves the praise. Well done, Gus!"

"Thank you, Dr. Noel."

Johnny was confused. "Why the 'well dones?' We lost the plans! The spy escaped!"

All three laughed.

Dr. Noel spoke. "No, Johnny. We did not lose the plans."

Chapter Twenty-Six

"I should say: We lost the plans. But they were plans we meant to lose." said Dr. Noel. "False plans. If the British try to build a submersible from it, it will sink."

"False plans?" asked Johnny. "Where are the real plans?"

"They are safe," said Dr. Noel.

Johnny said, "All this - the British sailors, the spy, the skiff - it was all to -"

Johnny's father burst through the door. An angry Vernon and a tussled Deane came behind.

"Pappa," started Johnny. "I —"

"Not now, Johnny," interrupted his father. "I have important news — Ben Franklin has signed a secret treaty with the King of France!"

"A secret treaty?" repeated Dr. Noel. "What is this secret treaty?"

"The captain of the French ship said Ben signed it months ago," said Johnny's father. "After the French heard about our victory at Saratoga, they signed it."

"Will the French give us ships?" asked Captain Tucker. "Arms? Soldiers?"

"I don't know. That part is secret, but the fact that it has been signed is not," said Johnny's father. "If it is true, the British will back away. We will have our freedom! The war will be over. That would mean our journey here was wasted. No need to have come to France." Johnny's father put an arm around Johnny and it came away wet. "What happened to you, son?"

Before Johnny could answer, Augusta spoke up. "I fell in the water, and Johnny jumped in to rescue me, Mr. Adams."

"What happened to Mr. Deane?" asked Johnny's father.

"Me, too," said Deane. "I fell in, too."

"Why was everyone falling in the water tonight?" asked Johnny's father.

Awkward glances circled the room. "Your son showed great courage," said Dr. Noel. "He acted selflessly and quickly and without a thought to himself."

Johnny was a little proud. But he was more afraid of what his father would say next.

"You're all right, son?" was all his father said.

"Yes, Pappa," said Johnny, wiping a drop of water from his forehead. "I'm all right."

"Good. Let's get you to bed. Tomorrow will be an important day. We'll get to Bordeaux and find someone who can tell us more about this secret treaty. If the job is done, we may sail back to America on the next ship."

Johnny wanted to ask more about the false secret plans Lord North's spy had taken, but Johnny went with his father to their cabin. He jumped into his hammock and wondered what the British would do when they learned of Dr. Noel's trick.

Lord North's spies were all over France, Dr. Noel had said. What would they do in Bordeaux? Would his father be in danger?

When Johnny woke the next morning, his father was gone. No light shone through the porthole. There was only a dark fog through the glass. Inside the wardrobe, all of his clothes were gone except a pair of breeches, a white shirt and a waistcoat. He put them on and climbed to the quarterdeck.

Daylight was burning off the fog and turning the stone buildings of Bordeaux pink on their way to white. On the docks, a trickle of workers soon became a stream. Boxes moved onto boats to be rowed to waiting ships. Space was made for arriving goods.

Augusta appeared at Johnny's elbow. "Ugh. Isn't this river water disgusting? It took me forever to wash it out of my hair last night. I miss the ocean already."

"I'd rather be on land," said Johnny.

Augusta laughed and held out a leather bag. "I bet you would. Here - this is for you. For carrying things."

"I can't give it back to you," said Johnny. "We're about to go to shore."

"I know," said Augusta. "It's a gift. For my rescuer."

Augusta blinked several times quickly.

"What are you doing?" asked Johnny.

"I'm batting my eyelashes," said Augusta. "Like ladies are supposed to do. For their rescuers."

"I didn't really rescue you," said Johnny. "Besides, you were rescuing Deane, so you were a rescuer, too."

"I don't think Deane is going to bat his eyelashes at me or you," laughed Augusta. "You'll have to settle for me." She blinked furiously. "Was that better?"

Deane ran up out of breath. "There you are! Are you ready to go to shore?"

"Yes, yes, of course," said Johnny, suddenly sad. "I guess I should say good-bye to you, Gus."

"I guess you should," said Augusta matter-of-factly. "But maybe you should say what Dr. Noel said: '*Au revoir.*'"

Til seen again, translated Johnny. "Will I see you again?"

"Perhaps," said Augusta mysteriously. "Perhaps when we're older, we'll see each other again."

Johnny was confused. "When we're older? Where?"

The awkward silence was too much for Deane. "Honestly, Johnny, is it that hard? She means she'd like to see you again. When you're both older."

Johnny still didn't get it. "Why does that matter?"

Deane laughed. "It *is* All Fool's Day, Johnny, but really. She's trying to say – Oh, never mind."

"Today is All's Fool's Day?" asked Johnny. With everything that had happened, he forgot it was April 1st.

Johnny felt like a fool. He had been a step behind

everything that happened. From the *Turtle* plans to Dr. Noel's plot to give the spy the wrong plans to not seeing Vernon's dangerous rage until it was almost too late. He felt like a fool.

"*Au revoir*, then, Johnny," said Augusta, brushing away a sudden moisture around her eyes. "Til I see you again!"

Captain Tucker grabbed Johnny by the shoulders. "Hey, Johnny, what's going on here? Something wrong?"

"No, I'm fine," said Johnny quickly. "I'm fine."

Captain Tucker took a long look at Augusta and Johnny and laughed. "I wanted to add my words to Dr. Noel's last night. You showed courage when it was needed. I thank you. Especially for pulling Gus here from the river."

Augusta batted her eyelashes again.

"You're welcome, Captain," said Johnny with embarrassment.

"To be serious, Johnny," said Captain Tucker. "I'd be happy to have you sail on my ship any time. Not quite ready to be an able-bodied sailor, but soon we'd get you there. And then, who knows? Maybe captain one day. Our navy could use you."

"He prefers the land, he says," said Augusta.

"Strange people everywhere, Gus," said Captain Tucker with a wink. "Strange people everywhere."

Vernon approached with a paper in his hand and said, "Captain, a word, if you please."

"As I was saying," said Captain Tucker. "How may

I help you, Mr. Vernon?"

"I should think you'd prefer to have this conversation in private," said Vernon.

"You can state your business here," said Captain Tucker.

Vernon was suddenly unsure of himself. "Well, then. If that's how you'd like it." He waved the sheet of paper in the air. "Here I have collected the many errors you made in captaining this vessel, beginning with the . . ."

Captain Tucker took the paper from Vernon's hand. "Thank you, Mr. Vernon. I appreciate your contribution."

"Give it back. I need to send that paper to my father," said Vernon, trying to grab the paper.

Captain Tucker handed the paper to Gus and stepped in front of Vernon. "Gus will make sure your paper goes where it should, won't you Gus?"

"Aye, aye, Captain," said Gus. She stepped to the rail and dropped it in the water. "I accidentally dropped it, Captain."

"That's all right, Gus," said Captain Tucker. "Those things happen."

Vernon stood to his full height. "I'll just write up another one and send it to my father."

Captain Tucker stepped within an inch of Vernon's face. "You should do that, Mr. Vernon. You should tell your father that you arrived safely in France after escaping a British man-of-war, sailing through a hurricane and arrived safely in Bordeaux.

You should tell him all of that. And when I'm back in America, I'll tell him exactly what a help you were on this journey. Especially when we had the British supply ship surrendered and you went to the forecastle to be sure the cannon was working."

"You —" Vernon shrunk back. "You've not heard the last of this."

Captain Tucker laughed.

Johnny's father emerged from the companion hatch with his bag. "All the books are boxed up. They'll go in the skiff with us. Anything else to do?"

"No, Pappa," said Johnny. "It's all done. Ready to go."

"Look at Bordeaux in the daylight," said Johnny's father. "Isn't it magnificent?"

Johnny wondered how much his father knew about the spy and what they had almost lost. Had anyone told him? "Pappa, about last night. Did they tell you what —"

From the other side of the ship, Dr. Noel called over. "Mr. Adams, do you think Johnny could come ashore with me? I could use his help."

Johnny's father nodded. "Of course. Johnny, go help Dr. Noel."

Dr. Noel was directing a large box into a longboat. Two sailors let out the rope. The suspended box dropped over the rail.

Deane said, "Can I go with you, too, Dr. Noel?"

"Only room for one," said Dr. Noel.

"Come with me, Mr. Deane," said Johnny's father.

"You'll come with me and Mr. Vernon. We'll see them on the dock."

Johnny followed Dr. Noel over the rope ladder and into the longboat. Dr. Noel perched himself on top of the box and put his long arms to the oars. Johnny pushed away from the *Boston* and held the box steady as Dr. Noel pulled the oars.

Johnny ran his fingers over the wood grain. It was a box he had seen in the hold. It was the box that Augusta had her doll in. But there had been other things in it, too. Gleaming, brassy things. The ship's parts, Augusta had said.

"Why are we taking ship's parts to shore?" asked Johnny.

"If you have answered the right questions, you should know," said Dr. Noel. "Questions about the enemy's greatest strength. Questions about the enemy's greatest fear," said Dr. Noel.

In a flash, Johnny knew what was in the box.

Chapter Twenty-Seven

In the box was a good thing.

In the box was a valuable thing.

But Johnny was worried.

The thing in the box was so valuable that Lord North's spies would kill for it.

Dr. Noel saw the worry in Johnny's eyes. "You asked me about the Committee, Johnny. Since you have shown you can help, would you like to know how I joined it?"

"What? Yes!" stammered Johnny.

"After I was healed by the Scot, I had two choices. One: rejoin the French army. Two: Choose a different battle."

"A different battle?"

"I chose a different battle. Then as always, there were many battles to choose from. Battles between powers. Battles between nations. Battles between men. Then there are the battles between men and sickness. Battles between men and death. A much more important kind of battle. I became a doctor," said Dr. Noel. "A soldier in the battle against sickness."

"What does being a doctor have to do with the Committee?"

"You cannot understand the end of a story without the beginning," said Dr. Noel patiently. "Are you ready to listen?"

"Yes," said Johnny.

"Good," said Dr. Noel. "The doctor's battle is a good battle, but it is a losing one. Because every patient dies. Maybe not today. Maybe not tomorrow. But eventually, every patient dies. Because every man dies. The best doctor cannot stop it. And doctors die, too."

Johnny remembered the day Dr. Warren died. The afternoon with Joey Warren watching the battle at Bunker Hill. It had been the third attack of the British soldiers. Dr. Warren had led the knot of soldiers who stopped the British from killing the escaping militia.

Doctors die, too.

"Being a doctor led me to a greater battle," continued Dr. Noel. "One that requires much sacrifice. A Committee was formed to fight this battle. In secret."

Johnny was confused. "What battle?"

"I should not call it a battle because it is bigger than that. It is a war. But a different kind of war. Different because most people do not believe it exists. Most people say, 'Might means right.' The strong make the rules. The weak follow. Important people command. Lesser people obey. Most people believe wars are between one king and another. One mighty man against another. Do you know the story of David and Goliath?"

"Of course," said Johnny.

"Tell me," said Dr. Noel.

"Goliath was a Philistine giant. When the Philistine army went to fight Israel, Goliath challenged a man of Israel to fight him."

"And Israel sent their strong man to fight him?"

"No - of course not," said Johnny. "They sent a shepherd boy - David."

"Indeed. A shepherd boy. Not a strong man. A weak boy," said Dr. Noel. "Who won?"

"David."

"How?"

"David used a sling. He hit Goliath in the forehead with the rock. Then he killed him."

"You see," said Dr. Noel. "The strongest man does not always win."

Johnny was confused. "What do David and Goliath have to do with the Committee?"

"There is a lie whispered in every heart, Johnny. It says, if you are strong enough, if you are powerful enough, if you know everything, you will be great. You will be like God. It is a lie as old as Adam and Eve. It comes to this, Johnny: Do you want to be God?"

Johnny laughed. "I'm sorry - I'm not - I'm just a boy! How could I be God?"

Dr. Noel smiled. "You say that now, but you will change. As you grow into a man, the lie will be whispered in your ear again and again. The whisper will urge you to become stronger than others. To become more powerful than others. To become a lord over others. The whisper will fill your thoughts. It will fill your dreams. Your every waking moment. It will tell you to become a lord above others."

Johnny shook his head. "Not me, Dr. Noel. A lord? I can't imagine."

"Someday, Johnny," said Dr. Noel with another pull on the oars. "Someday, you will want to obey it. More than anything. Because, secretly, in every human heart, there is the wish to be God."

Johnny ran his hand over the box. "But Dr. Noel, what about the Committee? What does any of this have to do with the Committee?"

"The Committee fights the way David fought," said Dr. Noel.

"With slings?" asked Johnny.

Dr. Noel smiled. "It wasn't a sling that defeated Goliath. It was David acting with faith. Last night, the battle was won by a boy and a girl. A boy and girl with courage who stopped Lord North's spy from taking Deane. And they protected a secret. The Committee fights with people, even the most unlikely people. Because the Committee has faith that a Sovereign Hand animates us all."

Johnny shook his head. It wasn't courage that made him do what he did. He had been afraid. Especially in the river. He hadn't felt courage. Only fear.

"We are almost at the dock, so you must tell me," said Dr. Noel. "What have you figured, as you say?

What is in the box?"

Johnny's fear returned. What would happen if Lord North's spies discovered it? How many more spies did the British have in France? Lord North's spies would do anything. Lord North's spies would hurt anyone to get a prize like this.

Then the fear left Johnny.

He was the boy with the girl who Dr. Noel had just talked about.

He was the boy with the girl who defeated the spy. He was the boy with the girl who rescued Deane. He was the boy with the girl who won.

It was a strange feeling. He had done exactly what he should have done. He was living the life he should live, as his mother had said. He was doing what was *right*.

Johnny traced the wood grain on the box. He knew why the box hadn't been touched by the ship's carpenter. He knew why Augusta had hidden her doll inside. She knew no one would look there because everyone had been told not to touch it.

It was a box with a mystery inside. A mystery he knew.

"The *Turtle* is in this box," said Johnny.

Dr. Noel pulled a last time on the oars. They drifted to the dock.

"In pieces, but yes," said Dr. Noel. "It is the *Turtle*. It is a small thing. Small like David's sling. Who knows? In the right hands, the *Turtle* may fell the giant ships of the British. We will take it to Dr. Franklin and see."

Historical Fact and Fiction

Sea Chase is historical fiction based on the true
story of young John Quincy Adams' trip to France in
1778. Here are the facts:

John Quincy Adams and Abigail Adams watched
the Battle of Bunker Hill (at the time, it was called
"Bunker's Hill" although most of the fighting was on
Breed's Hill) from Penn's Hill near Braintree (now
Quincy), Massachusetts. There is a stone called the
"Abigail Adams Cairn" that marks the spot. The
summer before the Battle at Bunker Hill, Dr. Joseph
Warren repaired John Quincy Adams' finger when
another doctor had recommended it be amputated.
Fifteen year-old Joseph Warren, Jr. was staying with
the Adams family the day his father fought at Bunker
Hill. Dr. Warren died stopping the third British
advance, allowing hundreds of Americans to escape.
In recognition of Dr. Warren's sacrifice, many towns
were named Warrenton and many counties were
named Warren County across the United States.

John and Johnny Adams left the Massachusetts
coast early on a misty morning in February 1778.
Their cousin Norton's wife Adelia gave the prophetic
statement about the dangers of their journey, with
John Adams writing that he was "not enough of a
Roman to believe it an ill omen."

202

Aboard Captain Samuel Tucker's *Boston*, the Adamses had a difficult journey. The *Boston* was chased by a British man-o-war, escaped into doldrums, and went through a hurricane in which it was struck by lightning and a sailor was killed. Lieutenant Barron was killed when the cannon firing a signal to a French ship exploded. He was buried at sea with the pieces of the cannon as weights.

Dr. Noel, a Frenchman returning from America, aided the hurt sailors and gave Johnny his first French lessons. The story of the Frenchman and the fleas is taken directly from the Autobiography of John Adams. He wrote:

One of Captain Tuckers Stories too diverted the Frenchmen as well as the Englishmen and Americans. A Frenchman in London Advertised an infallible Remedy against fleas. The Women as well as Men flocked to the place to purchase the Powder. But after many had bought it and paid for it, one only of the Women, asked for directions to Use it. Madam said the Frenchman, you must catch the Flea, and squeese him between your thumb and finger, till he gape, then put a little dust of this powder in his mouth, and he never will bite you again. But said the Lady when I have him between my fingers why may I not throw him in the fire or press him to death? Ah, Madam, said the Frenchman, dat will do just as well den.

Also aboard the *Boston* was Robert Vernon, Jr. Vernon was seventeen years old and a graduate of the College of New Jersey in Princeton, New Jersey, later

Princeton University. His Rhode Island family had been merchants, with Vernon's father and uncle Samuel shipping African slaves to South Carolina since 1737. When the war started, the British took the Vernon family's ships. Robert Vernon, Sr. moved to Boston and became President of the Eastern Navy Board, which was responsible for building and equipping ships of the Continental Navy, including the *Boston*.

Jesse Deane was twelve years old when he traveled aboard the *Boston* to meet his father Silas Deane in France.

The *Turtle* was the first submarine ever put into military action, built by Yale graduate David Bushnell in 1775. It was used against British ships in the Hudson River outside New York City in 1776. In 1777, the *Turtle* disappeared. No one knows what happened to it. There is no record of the *Turtle* being aboard the *Boston*, but there probably wouldn't have been a record, if it was.

Johnny and his father arrived in Bordeaux on April 1st, 1778 and learned what the secret treaty between France and the United States meant.

In France, Johnny's adventures continued.

If you enjoyed *Sea Chase*,
think of a friend who would enjoy it.

Please let them know.

More by John Braddock:

Fiction:
The 24th Name

Non-fiction:
A Spy's Guide To Thinking
A Spy's Guide To Strategy

Made in the USA
Monee, IL
24 May 2022